A Child's Journey into Yoga

Stories, Wisdom & Activities
Based on the Core Sutras of Patanjali

Written by
Lydia Nitya Griffith

Illustrated by
Bella Nathanson, age 11

A Child's Journey into Yoga:
Stories, Wisdom & Activities Based on the Core Sutras of Patanjali
Written by Lydia Nitya Griffith

Illustrated by Bella Nathanson
Edited & Designed by Ian F. Wesley

The Arrival Media

Richmond, Virginia, United States
www.TheArrivalMedia.com

First Edition
ISBN 978-0-9905505-1-8

Key Words

Yoga	Youth Fiction	Character-Building	Healthy Living
Sutras of Patanjali	Sri Swami Satchidananda		Yogaville

Disclaimer
The sayings of The Man with the Long White Beard in this book are paraphrases (rather than quotes) of Sri Swami Satchidananda as interpreted by the author.

DEDICATION

To my eternal teacher,
Sri Swami Satchidananda,
and to all the many children
who have taught me the joy
of teaching yoga.

CONTENTS

PART 1   HEARING THE GURU

NOTE FROM THE AUTHOR

When I hear my yoga name, Nitya, it is a reminder of why I am here. My desires to create, to write, and to help others came together through yoga.

I had the good fortune of taking the Integral Yoga Teacher Training in 2005 with Nora Vimala Pozzi in Richmond, Virginia. The training cracked me wide open to see all the darkness, light, ugliness, and beauty that was me. It was one of the most difficult passages of my life and one of the most transformative.

My connection to Sri Swami Satchidananda, founder of Integral Yoga, is a constant motivation to serve with an open heart. His desire to share yoga with children inspired me to continue his mission. I have discovered a passion for teaching children, from the adorable two-year-olds up to the independent twelve-year-olds. Through yoga, I encourage them to peek into themselves as they study with me, and I have absolute faith that their lives will be far easier because of what they discover.

When I am sitting in a class of children, I feel like I am eight years old, and I relate to them at their level, and we connect. I have been teaching children's yoga classes since 2005. In each class, together we plant seeds of yoga wisdom. Hundreds of children have participated in my annual Yoga with Nitya Summer Camp for Kids and Teens, which provides an immersive, forty-hour weekly experience of living yoga in which those seeds take root. I also offer teacher training for children's yoga (*visit* YogaWithNitya.com).

Yoga is a journey of discovering your True Self. I often tell my children that "OM" is in the center of the word "home" and is a reminder to come home to

yourself. If I achieve nothing else in my life, I hope to inspire as many children as I can to honor themselves, to treat others with compassion, and to love and treasure this beautiful world we all share and call hOMe.

Illustrator

Bella Nathanson studied yoga with me more than five years prior to illustrating this book at the age of eleven. The process of working with Bella was another joyous and challenging yoga adventure, an education for both teacher and student.

Bella also appears in my children's yoga DVD, *Yoga with Nitya*, coproduced by Emmy Award winner Roberta Oster Sachs.

INTRODUCTION

Patanjali means "an offering who fell from heaven." He was the author of the sutras, the ancient Sanskrit teachings, on which yoga is based. Many say he is the Father of Yoga. In all my years of teaching children's yoga classes and summer camps, I searched for books that convey the principles and values found in the yoga sutras. Eventually, I realized that what was missing was a book for children that encapsulates the core teachings of Patanjali. It is from Patanjali and the guiding voice of Sri Swami Satchidananda that I drew these teachings for children.

According to legend, Patanjali was half man and half serpent. He had four arms: two hands were held together at his heart, one hand held the wheel of time or the law of karma, in his fourth hand he held a conch shell that contained the universal sound of OM. When it is time to practice our yoga, OM is the sound that calls us to pay attention.

Sit in *sukkaasana* (cross legged) with a nice, straight back, close your eyes, and take a deep breath in and exhale with a gentle OM. Feel the vibration of OM moving through your body.

Let's do that again.
Deep breath, exhale OM.

Now you are ready to begin.

PART I

HEARING THE GURU

CHAPTER 1

WHAT YOU FOCUS ON EXPANDS

The man with the long white beard says:

"My friends, everything you think, that is what your life will be. What you focus on expands."

Mica was at school, and her third grade teacher, Mrs. Swan, sent her to the storage room to get a broom. Mica was a fearful person and became scared very easily. She was afraid of many things, such as being bullied in school, chased by the neighbor's dog, and the gym teacher who yelled a lot. Mica didn't want to go to the storage room. Her heart began to beat faster as she got closer to the door, and her hands were so sweaty she could barely grip the door knob.

As she opened the door, Mica's eyes were wide open and her heart beat so loudly it sounded like drums in her ears. In her mind she had created so much fear that she was consumed with it. Just as Mica flicked on the light switch, a mouse scurried across the floor and over her shoe. Mica let out a scream, grabbed the broom, and ran breathlessly back to her classroom.

Mrs. Swan heard the story Mica told of the mouse, but Mrs. Swan could also see how Mica's fearfulness created a scary situation. So, she asked Mica to stay after school with her.

"Mica, your thoughts create what happens in your life. By expecting something frightful, you are actually making yourself scared. I tell you what, let's do some artwork." Mrs. Swan handed Mica some crayons and a piece of paper. "What do you think the opposite of fearful is?"

Mica said, "Brave."

"That is right. So I want you to draw me a picture of you being brave."

When Mica was finished, Mrs. Swan taped the picture to Mica's desk. Every day that she saw the brave girl in the picture, Mica felt braver inside herself. Over time, Mrs. Swan noticed Mica sitting up straighter, looking people in the eyes when she spoke to them, and it was easier for Mica to get the broom from the storage room for clean-up time.

Mica found that the more she thought of bravery, the more experiences she had being brave. She found herself standing up to the class bully, meeting the neighbor's dog with a treat, and breathing calmly when the gym teacher yelled. Mica was learning that seeing herself as brave was helpful and that ultimately whatever thoughts she had really did change how she felt, and sometimes even what would happen.

CLASS ACTIVITY

Have students think about an uncomfortable feeling they often have in certain situations (for example: being fearful on the diving board, shy around new people, awkward when raising one's hand in class, or getting angry when you don't get your way).

Now ask them to think of the opposite of that feeling under the same circumstances. Using paper and colored pencils, have them draw self-portraits showing themselves embodying the desired traits.

CHAPTER 2

CALMING THE MIND

The man with the long white beard says:

"Your mind is like a crystal clear pool of water. Each thought is like a pebble dropped in the pool creating ripples. Many thoughts make many ripples. We practice yoga to stop the ripples, to stop all the pebbles of thoughts, so our minds can be still and clear.

When your mind is totally clear, totally still, totally focused on this Now moment, you will be

free. *This clear and still state of mind is called* samadhi. *Controlling the mind and its thoughts is one of the most important teachings of yoga.*"

Sanskrit word
Samadhi
"enlightenment"

Mica came home from school and sat down at the kitchen table to do her homework. Her little brother was watching television, her mom was talking to a client on the phone, and Mica's mind was busy. She heard all these distractions while still full of the experiences from school.

Mica struggled to focus on her math homework and decided to try to calm her mind by moving upstairs to her quiet bedroom.

Sitting on her bed with the door closed, Mica felt all the distractions from downstairs melt away, and soon her school day faded into the distance, too. She lay down on her bed and followed her breathing as her tummy rose and fell. After a while, Mica felt a calm peacefulness growing inside of her. Mica was learning that by stilling her mind she could be focused, calm, and peaceful. Mica smiled and gave herself a hug. And she then found that her math was much easier to do.

CLASS ACTIVITY

Fill a large glass bowl with water. Explain that this is like the mind in its natural state. Next, explain that pebbles represent our thoughts. Drop a few pebbles in the water and explain that the ripples from the pebbles of thoughts disturb the tranquility of the mind. Ask what they think would help return the mind to stillness.

Meditating is one tool to quiet the mind, another is breathing mindfully. Ask how Mica stilled her mind. She followed her breath.

Now have the students lie on their backs. Ask them to rest their hands on their stomachs. Encourage them to notice that while breathing in the tummy rises; breathing out, the tummy falls. Now, ask them to close their eyes and continue to feel their breath rising and falling. This is a very good way to introduce meditation.

CHAPTER 3

WE ARE ALL CONNECTED

The man with the long white beard says:

"We are all threads in the fabric of life, one giant quilt for all living beings. There's me, there's you, and you and you and you, and all the elephants, tigers, monkeys, ants, trees, roses, dandelions. You see? All of life is breathing: plants, trees, animals, insects, and humans.

You must know then, that whatever you do, whatever you think, whatever you say affects many living things around you. We are all connected."

Mica got up from her bed and went downstairs, lured by the aroma of dinner cooking. "I'm hungry!" she declared as she walked into the kitchen.

"Well, I just got started, and it won't be ready for a while," her mom replied.

Mica was irritated, because she wanted to eat right away. Suddenly, all the peacefulness she felt earlier in her room was gone. She insisted, "But, Mom, I'm *really* hungry!"

Mica's mom turned around and said calmly, "Mica, I'm hungry, too, so is your brother and, judging from the empty bowl on the floor, so is the dog."

Mica stopped and heard her mother's words. Mica realized she wasn't any more hungry or important than anyone else in the house. Everyone was hungry, and everyone wanted dinner. So she decided the least she could do was feed the dog. Mica spent the rest of her time waiting for dinner by setting the table and helping to make the salad. When everyone was seated, Mica realized how they had all been hungry together and now they were all eating together, just like they were all breathing together and living together as a family. Mica then understood there are millions of families just like hers who are all connected as one big Earth family.

"Mica, whatcha smilin' about?" her brother asked.

"Just seeing the you in me and the me in you," she said softly.

CLASS ACTIVITY

Ask the students to sit in a large circle. Roll a ball of yarn across the circle to someone while holding on to the end. Have the students continue rolling the ball of yarn to others while holding the strand. Tell them they are making a web.

Continue rolling the ball of yarn until each person is holding a strand. Now ask them to stand up. Discuss how the web they've created connects everyone. Relate this to different scenarios where, in a team or ecosystem, losing one person or species disrupts the balance of the whole.

CHAPTER 4

WHO ARE YOU?

The man with the long white beard declares:

"Your Spirit Self is unchanging, it is indestructible, it is everlasting. So then, how do you see your self?"

Mr. Lee was the substitute teacher for the third grade class while Mrs. Swan was out for the week. He didn't yell like some teachers. He did not send misbehaving kids to the principal. All through the first day, Mr. Lee was calm, patient, and accepting of the students as they were. Mica watched Mr. Lee closely and with a bit of wonderment. She couldn't imagine how he could put up with some of the students' behavior all week long.

Tuesday, Mr. Lee came into the room and without a word motioned with his hand, and the kids all sat in their seats. Mr. Lee told them, "Class, please open your notebooks and write this question: 'Who am I?' And then answer it. Take your time, and yes, it will count for a grade."

Some of the kids laughed at the assignment, thinking it was stupid. Others were totally perplexed and didn't know how to begin, but Mica felt something stirring inside her that gave her the confidence to meet this challenge.

Mr. Lee collected the papers and read them while the class went to music. Some kids had given simple answers, such as where they lived, about their families, the sports they played, or what they liked. When Mr. Lee came to Mica's paper, he smiled. Mica had written a poem:

Mica is soft like the wind.

Mica is still and quiet.

Mica is the sky filled with clouds of thoughts.

Mica is the song of birds and the wail of the wolf.

Mica is a part of the world.

Mica is me.

Mr. Lee sat with Mica at lunch. "How did you decide on your answer in today's writing assignment?"

"I guess, I just see my-self as a part of the world around me." Mica said quietly, "I feel like somehow we are all connected. What I do could affect many people. What I think can make things more likely to happen. What I feel can make it easier or harder to think clearly. I've been paying more attention to myself lately."

Mr. Lee asked her more questions about her own feelings and her view of the world.

Mica also shared with Mr. Lee her earlier incident with the mouse in the storeroom and the drawing activity that Mrs. Swan had given to help her to overcome her anxiety. Mica was surprised by how easy it was to talk to Mr. Lee. She couldn't remember any adult she could open up to like this, and she found it both strange and wonderful.

Mr. Lee smiled warmly at Mica, "Have you ever taken a Hatha yoga class before?"

"No. What's Hatha yoga?"

"In my Hatha yoga class, we do gentle stretching, meditation, and breathing in order to have a healthier body and a more peaceful mind. I teach a 4:00 Monday class at Sunrise Yoga Studios on Harmony Boulevard. Here, I brought you an enrollment form." He handed the paper to Mica and said, "See if your parents will sign you up. The class is for older kids, but I think you'll fit right in."

Sanskrit word
Hatha
It's what you do on a yoga mat.

Mica thought Mr. Lee was the best substitute teacher ever. She'd never had someone listen to her like that before or ask her those deep, thoughtful questions. Somehow, Mica knew Mr. Lee had come into her life for a reason and that he was there to teach her something important. The first step, though, was to convince her parents to let her take the class.

When Mica got home from school, she ran inside to tell her mom all about Mr. Lee. "Mom! I have something to tell you!" Mica yelled, letting the screen door slam shut behind her.

Mica's mom came out of the living room, "Hi, how was your day? What is all this excitement?"

"I have the nicest substitute teacher, Mr. Lee, this week. He gave me this flyer about a yoga class he teaches. Can I go, Mom?" Mica handed her the flyer. They walked together into the kitchen and sat down at the table.

"Oh, Mica, your dad really wants you to try out for the soccer team. You two talked about that this summer. Don't you want to play a sport and do something active? What is this *yoga* anyway?"

Mica felt her heart sink and disappointment set in. She began to gather her things and head out of the room.

"Now hold on, Mica. Sit down and tell me why this is so important to you."

So Mica sat down and told her mom about her writing assignment, how Mr. Lee had responded to it, and how she believed Mr. Lee had selected her to attend this yoga class. "Plus, Mom, it's an older kids' class, and he thinks I would be good in it," Mica added, daring to look up and meet her mom's eyes.

With a deep sigh, Mica's mom said, "Well, I know several people who take classes at the Sunrise Yoga Studio, and I think it's a great idea that they offer a kids' yoga class. I don't know much about yoga, but I am going to say yes. You obviously are really excited about the idea of learning yoga. But, you still should talk to your dad about the soccer team."

"Thanks, Mom!" Mica ran upstairs, leaping two steps at a time. She was so happy.

That night after dinner, Mica spoke with her dad about the yoga classes and Mr. Lee. He looked at her with a questioning squint in his warm, brown eyes.

"I wonder about the soccer team you were going to try out for, Mica. What about that? And tell me about this yoga?"

"Well, Mr. Lee told me it's a class with stretching and meditation. Is it alright that I changed my mind? I mean, I don't want to disappoint you, Daddy." Mica sat in her dad's lap and gave him a big hug.

"Oh, you are my girl! You melt my heart every time. Go learn your yoga. Go." Her father gave her a warm hug and a kiss on her forehead.

At that moment, Mica remembered her life in Nebraska and how her grandmother, Ravenwalk, would kiss her just like that. They would have brought Ravenwalk with them when they moved to Virginia, but she was too old and frail and didn't want to move. Mica really missed her grandmother and had been writing to her to stay in touch.

As Mica turned to go upstairs to bed, she said to her mom and dad, "Don't worry, I will tell you all about yoga after my first class with Mr. Lee. Good night!"

CLASS ACTIVITY

Hand out journals to the students. Instruct them to choose a specific time each day to stop and write in the journals for self-reflection. As a first assignment, have them write "Who Am I?" at the top of the page and answer the question.

Suggested reading: *I Am: Why Two Little Words Mean So Much* by Dr. Wayne W. Dyer with Kristina Tracy.

CHAPTER 5

FINDING THE TRUTH

The man with the long white beard says:

"Now there are three ways to get to the Truth. First, you can see it for yourself, which is called direct perception. *Second is* inference, *and that means that if, for example, you saw smoke in the woods, you may assume there is a fire. The third is* learned, *which should come from a reliable source, like unbiased news or a respected teacher.*

Remember, though, when drawing conclusions and gathering information, to make sure your mind is clear from fear, judgment, or attachment."

Sarah and Mica had known each other since the beginning of the school year, when Mica moved to Northern Virginia from Nebraska. When Mica first came to Sparks School, everyone thought she was quiet and different.

Sarah started a rumor one day on the playground. She whispered to Laurel, "You know Mica is an Indian name. Mica must be an immigrant. I don't think she knows English very well. Maybe that's why she's so quiet."

In gym class, Laurel told Jake, "That new girl Mica is from Indonesia and doesn't speak English."

Jake was surprised to hear this. "Wow, that's weird!" So Jake told his buddy Will on the bus ride home, "Dude, that girl Mica is from some country in Asia and doesn't speak much English."

Will happened to live next door to Mica; he turned to Jake and asked, "How do you know that's true?"

Jake shrugged his shoulders, "I dunno, Laurel told me."

Will went home and called Laurel. He found out that she had heard the rumor from Sarah. So Will called Sarah. "Hey, Sarah, what's this I hear about Mica being from Asia and not knowing English?"

"What?! I didn't say that! I said *India*."

"Why do you think that?" asked Will. "I'm just curious."

"Um, I dunno. She has brownish-red skin and black hair. Plus she hardly says anything, so she probably doesn't know much English. Right? Weird, huh?" Sarah was starting to feel uncomfortable.

"Well, you know, Mica lives next door to me, right?"

Now feeling even worse, Sarah mumbled, "No, I didn't know that."

"Will you do me favor, then? Would you ask Mica tomorrow at school about where she's from? Maybe you should get to know her first before talking about her behind her back. Just sayin', ya know."

Sarah's stomach churned into a twisted knot. She had spread lies about someone she knew nothing about. Just because she had assumed that Mica must be foreign, because she was quiet, had dark skin and black hair, did not make that necessarily true.

The next day, Sarah sat with Mica at recess. "Hi, Mica. I'm Sarah, I sit a few rows behind you in class."

"Hi." Mica was shy and timid. She was still working on being more brave and confident.

"So, like, where are you from?"

In perfect English, Mica said, "I'm from an Indian reservation in Nebraska. We moved here last summer because my dad got a job in D.C."

"Oh," Sarah said flatly, "so you're a Native American?"

Mica nodded.

Sarah got up and said, "Excuse me, I think I have to fix something before it becomes a big problem." Then Sarah went to each person she had told that rumor to and set the record straight.

That day, Sarah and her friends learned a lesson about getting information directly from a *reliable* source before assuming what they first heard or saw was the truth. Asking Mica directly was the right thing to do, and Sarah felt better for doing that.

CLASS ACTIVITY

Gossip Train is a great way to instill the importance of telling the truth, not gossiping, but getting facts from a reliable source. Have students sit in a circle and choose one person to start a silly rumor, such as, "I saw a pink gorilla dancing on a mini van in the school parking lot," and whisper it to the next person. Each person in turn should whisper the rumor they heard to the next person until everyone has heard the rumor. Finally, ask the last person to say out loud what she or he heard. The rumor is seldom the same at the end than it was at the start, and this is the point of the lesson.

CHAPTER 6

THE PRACTICE OF YOGA

The man with the long white beard says:

"My little yogis, your yoga practice must be firmly a part of your daily life. You must not take a break from it. You should always feel great joy in your practice."

Mica was so excited when that following Monday came, because she would soon take her first yoga class. She made sure to wear clothes that allowed her to move around easily, and she wore a hair clip to pull her long, black hair off of her face.

That afternoon, when they arrived at the yoga studio, Mica's mom handed her a brand new yoga mat in a carry bag. "Here, Honey, I got you a little present. I am so proud of you for accepting all the changes we've gone through this year with such maturity and for how you've embraced your new life here in Virginia." Mica's mom gave her a hug.

"Thanks, Mom! Oh, a yoga mat, and it's my favorite color, orange! You're the best." Mica got out of the car and headed into the Sunrise Yoga Studio.

Mr. Lee was waiting on his purple yoga mat when Mica walked into the large room. There were about ten other kids on mats, too. Mica unrolled her mat with a sudden "snap!" and blushed at the loud noise she'd made. Everyone looked startled but then smiled at her.

Mica sat on her mat and listened to Mr. Lee's soft voice guiding them to do various poses or *asanas*. The kids in the class were a little older and had taken this class for a while. Mica was a bit intimidated by how well they all knew the poses and she tried her best to keep up.

She went to class faithfully for twelve weeks (that's three months). Soon she was able to do all of the asanas with ease and she could sit in meditation focusing on her breath for a full ten minutes. But, as time went by, Mica found herself getting bored with the routine of the class.

One Monday, Mica lied and told her mom she had a stomach ache and didn't feel up to going to class. The next week she said she had too much homework. The third week she admitted, "Mom, I don't want to go back to yoga class. I'm kind of bored with it."

Mr. Lee missed having Mica in class and wondered why she suddenly stopped attending. At the Saturday farmer's market he ran into Mica shopping with her mom.

"Hey, Mica! How have you been? We've missed having you in class," Mr. Lee said reaching out to hug Mica.

Mica accepted his hug, not wanting to admit she'd missed his class, too. She looked down at her shoes and mumbled, "I don't think I like yoga anymore."

Mica's mom gasped, "Mica, don't be rude! Look at Mr. Lee when you are talking to him."

Mr. Lee asked Mica, "What did you want to happen in class?"

"I dunno. I just thought there would be more to it. We always do the same thing."

"Hmmm, well, that's why we call it yoga *practice*. We are practicing to get better." Mr. Lee continued, "Did you do any of the practice at home like I suggested?"

"Not really. Sometimes, like when I was bored, I'd try to do some."

"Well, most of the kids in your class have been with me for years. Some started when they were five or six years old. They've learned that yoga practice is something they must really enjoy doing, that they need to do it every day, and never take a break from it, even if they're sick or on vacation. You will learn, Mica, that when you have that level of dedication, yoga becomes a part of who you are, and you will love it."

"Wow, I had no idea," Mica said, surprised by the level of dedication her classmates had and the commitment they were making to the practice.

"So, do this, Mica," Mr. Lee looked at Mica's mom for approval. "Try spending the next week doing your practice at home every day. Then, when you are ready, come back to class and see if you notice a difference."

Mica's mom nodded to him and looked at Mica with a smile. Mica nodded as well. Everyone knew what she was agreeing to. Mica's eyes sparkled with renewed excitement. "Mr. Lee, we will be seeing you soon. Thank you so much." Mica's mom said.

"Namaste," Mr. Lee said, bringing his hands to his heart and bowing.

When Mica got home, she decided she would set her alarm clock thirty minutes earlier so she could do a few asanas and some meditation before school. She would focus on her favorite poses of the shoulder stand, fish,

Sanskrit word
Namaste
a greeting, meaning:
"the light in me sees the light in you"

child's pose, sleeping swan, and the sun salutation. She sat in her favorite chair by her bedroom window and meditated on the sounds of the morning song-birds, the wind in the trees, and the chorus of dogs barking up the sun in the neighborhood. Mica was surprised by the growing calm within her each passing day. She felt less anxious and more confident, too.

After ten days, Mica was back in yoga class. She realized that yoga wasn't something she could do effectively once or twice a week. Just like brushing her teeth once or twice a week wouldn't be enough to prevent cavities. So Mica decided to commit fully to her practice, with enthusiasm, practicing every morning at six o'clock with no excuses to interrupt her routine. She stuck with it even when she went on sleepovers, was sick with the flu, and even when her family went on vacation.

Gradually, Mica began to notice all the wonderful benefits of yoga: she was healthier, calmer, more focused, she overcame problems more easily, and she had a growing feeling of inner peace. Some kids at school would tease, "Hey, Mica, what's that goofy grin on your face?!"

And Mica would continue to hold her gentle smile thinking, "If only you knew. I'm smiling from the inside."

Mica stopped looking for each class to be something new or entertaining. She accepted that even when class was the same, it was Mr. Lee's way of helping them master each pose. She now understood that, over time, making yoga part of her daily life would reveal all the magical benefits of the practice.

Mica's mom enrolled her in a summer yoga camp taught by Miss Nitya, checked out books on yoga from the library, and for spring break, the whole family went on a yoga retreat to Hawaii. After that, Mica's parents and even her younger brother were getting into yoga. All these experiences and new information increased Mica's love of yoga and reinforced her passion to practice.

CLASS ACTIVITY

For one week, have students write each day in their journals about their practice. They can choose a set number of asanas. Ask them to record what they experienced physically, emotionally, and spiritually in each of the poses. They should try to hold the poses for several minutes for optimum results. At the end of the week, have a sharing circle to discuss how this level of focus enhanced the benefits of their practice.

CHAPTER 7

DESIRE CAUSES SUFFERING

"Attachment comes from wanting, and wanting comes from believing you are separate from everyone else. But, my friends, there is no me without you. And so, why should I cling to something or someone for myself when there is everyone else to consider?" **asks the old man, stroking his long white beard.**

One Monday, Mr. Lee told his class that he would be traveling to India for a retreat and would be gone for three months. Mica felt many emotions flood her mind and body: anxiety over what would happen to *her* class, sadness over losing *her* teacher for so long, and anger at Mr. Lee for abandoning *her*. Mica was so overcome, she got up from her mat and ran out of the room in tears. Some of the other students were also upset.

Mr. Lee called everyone back to their mats and said gently, "My friends, I am not deserting you. In order for me to continue serving with all the work that I do, I must take time to nurture myself." He picked up the water pitcher on the desk behind him and continued, "A pitcher can only quench your thirst when it is full. If we pour out all the water, what is left to give?" He put the pitcher down and sat back on his mat.

"I have asked Miss Nitya, whom many of you know from summer yoga camp, to substitute teach for me starting next week."

To ease the heavy energy the students were feeling, Mr. Lee led the class in using *pranayama* or breath control to release the tension. "Please, sit up straight, close your eyes and take three deep breaths, releasing each breath with a gentle 'ahh' sound."

Then Mr. Lee began the class again, but this time he didn't focus on the asanas, he spoke instead of the teachings of yoga. "It is important that you understand this," he began, "controlling your monkey mind is the root practice of yoga. Why do you think that is so?"

Joey raised his hand, "Mr. Lee, I have a *human* mind, not a monkey mind!"

"Ah, true, Joey, but who here remembers what the monkey mind refers to?"

Sanskrit word
Pranayama
"breath control"

Shanti jumped in to say, "Monkeys are all over the place, just like our minds. It's hard to stop the mind from constantly thinking or being distracted."

Aida added, "Yeah, and I think what Mr. Lee is saying is that the goal of yoga is to stop the monkey mind by controlling our thoughts. Isn't that what we're doing in meditation?"

"Very good," said Mr. Lee smiling. "So, with the mind controlled, you discover your True Self."

"Yeah, Mr. Lee, I've had times meditating when my mind seems to stop and there's this emptiness, like a big vacuum of space that opens up. But then the feeling passes," Joey shared.

"Why do you think the moment was lost?" Mr. Lee asked.

"I think because I was looking at it."

"You became attached to it because it felt good. Whenever something feels good, we wish to experience it over and over again. Like, for example, some people recall the exhilarating rush of roller coasters when they think of amusement parks, and want to ride the rides over and over again. For others, however, it brings up awful memories of getting sick on a ride, and they don't want to experience it again. When we say something brings pleasure or pain, we've attached ourselves to it with conditions, judgments and opinions."

Mica chimed in, "I know how that feels. My family loves to go to Wild Jerry's Amusement Park, but I always get sick. Last time I just sat on the bench holding everyone's drink. It was so boring."

"Mica, did you ever think that the way you felt was selfish?" Mr. Lee asked.

"Huh?! *No!* I was the one dragged there who didn't want to go in the first place."

"Okay, now think like a yogi. What would a yogi do in this situation?"

Lily answered, "I think you have to remove yourself from where you are."

"Ah, now we're getting somewhere. Who knows what Lily is saying?"

"Oooh, I know!" Joey said excitedly, "If Mica went to the park as a *service* to her family, she'd have a whole new experience."

"Okay, and what might that be?" Mr. Lee prodded.

Joey continued, "If you had to do something you didn't want to do or didn't like doing, you could focus instead on the people you are with. Holding their drinks would be an act of *karma* yoga. You may even find yourself laughing and having a good time, just by sharing in the experience."

Mr. Lee said, "This is the difference between thinking selfishly and thinking about the well-being of others. Life is not about being attached to things, people, and experiences only because you find them pleasurable. Peace of mind comes from rising above selfish thinking. This way you experience the meaning of yoga."

Sanskrit word
Karma
Service to others without seeking any reward

Mr. Lee asked the class, "Where does true happiness come from?"

The students answered in unison, "Inside of me!"

Mr. Lee concluded, "So don't be attached to the idea that this is *your* class or I am *your* teacher. Everything good in this world is right there inside of you: peace, love, joy, contentment, gratitude, compassion. Do not long for a specific outcome. Do not hope for rewards. Do not wish for things to be different. Just you being you is all you need to be. Follow this, and you will find your practice deepens, and it becomes easier to live yoga off the mat in your daily life."

Mr. Lee put his hands together at his heart, smiled and bowed. "Namaste, friends, I will see you in a few months."

CLASS ACTIVITY

The goal for this activity is to move past attachment, judgment and self-oriented thinking.

Have the students spend a week doing one thing every day that they really don't like to do, while eliminating one thing they do like to do. For example, doing chores around the house might be something they don't like to do and watching TV might be something they do like to do. They should record in their journals each day what took place and how they felt about it. At the end of the week, break the students into groups for them to share their experiences.

CHAPTER 8

THE FOUR LOCKS AND FOUR KEYS

The man with the long white beard explains, *"People behave in four kinds of ways: happy, unhappy, virtuous, and wicked. You must use the right approach with people based on their behavior, the same way you must use the right key for every door. Choosing the wrong key for a door results in frustration; choosing the correct key brings peace, and is the way of yoga.*

The four keys *are friendliness, compassion, delight, and disregard. Watch as Mica encounters the four doors of behavior and learns how to choose the right key."*

Mica had made a good friend in yoga class. Lily was twelve, and Mica felt very special to have such a mature, older friend. Lily invited Mica to the mall after school to hang out. Mica was so excited she had her mom drop her off early at the Mega Mart. She waited a while and then saw Lily approaching. What she didn't expect to see was Lily walking with another friend her age. They were laughing and appeared to be having a good time. As they joined up and walked together, Mica began to feel more like a little sister tagging along.

Mica was really struggling with her feelings, but then she remembered this was her good friend from yoga class. She smiled from the inside. Just then, Lily looked at Mica and said, "I'm really glad we're hanging out together."

Mica's smile grew as she said, "Me, too."

Then Mica realized that **Being Friendly is the Key to the Door of Happy People**. If Mica envied the happiness Lily had with another friend, she'd lose her peace to jealousy. By being friendly with them, their happiness grew and everyone could have a good time.

The next day, Mica went to school and was confronted with a dilemma. A boy named Isaiah was paired up with her in gym class. Isaiah was not an athletic boy; in fact, he was known to be the slowest kid in class. Mica thought what a bummer it was to have this boy for her partner, and Isaiah wasn't looking any happier. Mica wondered why he wasn't glad to be teamed up with someone as limber and speedy as she.

As they did their stretches and worked through the drills, Isaiah became more and more upset. Mica saw he actually had tears in his eyes. Mica was then glad he was her partner, because she didn't think anyone else in her class would do what she was about to do. Mica began to open her heart and feel compassion for Isaiah.

"Hey, Isaiah, can I help you out with this stretch?" Mica asked softly.

Relieved, Isaiah said, "Yes, that would be great. I get so frustrated trying to get my body to do these exercises."

Mica smiled and meant it when she said, "I'm glad I got partnered up with you, Isaiah. You're a really nice person."

Isaiah smiled back.

Mica realized **Compassion is the Key to the Door of Unhappy People.** By choosing compassion for Isaiah instead of resenting his weakness, she preserved her inner peace and helped ease his frustrations, too.

Mica was so happy with herself after gym, that when the opportunity came up again in science class, she chose Isaiah for her partner. They had to work on a project together about planets. Over the next week, they would need to construct a model of the solar system. He was really good at science, but Mica struggled with the subject.

Isaiah had an idea involving clay and bamboo sticks, which Mica didn't want to do. Her idea was to use balloons and string, but Isaiah kept insisting

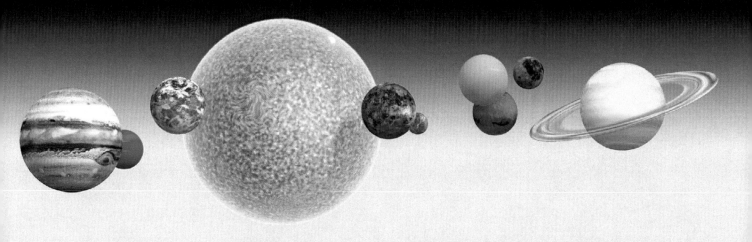

his way was better. As he explained to her why he disagreed, she didn't really listen. Because Isaiah wouldn't agree to her idea, she didn't really consider his, and didn't do much to help, either.

Isaiah's mom bought all the supplies, and on the next day, Isaiah brought them to class along with a sketch of the finished project for them to follow. Mica became more upset, so much so that she suspected her attitude about the situation was probably why she had lost her inner peace.

As Isaiah worked, he talked a lot about space, the solar system, his trips to the NASA Space Center in Florida, and all the books he had on science. Mica began to think that while he may not be the fastest kid in class, he sure did love science and knew a lot about the subject. She came to understand Isaiah did have the better idea. Instead of being annoyed with his knowledge, she realized she should have been cooperating and contributing all along.

Friendliness

Compassion

Delight

Disregard

"Mica, are you just going to sit there staring at me or are you going to help me out?" Isaiah asked, looking at her. "Here, why don't you work on the description cards? Your handwriting is much better than mine, and you're better with words, too."

Mica began to enjoy working on the project, and as she designed the description cards, she checked in with Isaiah for suggestions and ideas. In the end, they found it was fun working together, and they constructed an excellent model of the solar system. Mica had also learned a lot about space by watching and listening to Isaiah.

Mica discovered that **Delight is the Key to the Door of the Virtuous.** Isaiah's love and knowledge of science were *good things* or virtues. For two days Mica had been miserable, wanting to get her way, when she could have had more fun by listening to and appreciating Isaiah's knowledge from the beginning.

At the end of the school day, she was getting onto the bus when the class bully, Fisher, tripped her, and she fell, scraping her chin on the pavement. Mica lay there, feeling the sting of the cut and anger at the boy who had done it. He just stood over her laughing.

Happy   Sad   Virtuous   Wicked

Mica yelled at him, "Fisher! Walk like a normal person and keep your stupid feet to yourself!"

The boy said, "I can walk just fine, *you're* the klutz that tripped over your own two feet!"

Mica was even angrier now, and shouted, "I did *not* trip over my own two feet! *You* tripped *me*, and you know it!"

"Did not, you liar!" Fisher shouted back.

Before Mica could do or say anything back to Fisher, Sarah came over and said to her, "You'll get nowhere arguing with him. Just get up and walk away."

Sarah helped Mica get on the bus.

As Mica rode home, she thought to herself about what had happened. "Sarah was right. By ignoring Fisher's mean behavior I would have kept my own peace."

Disregard is the Key to the Door of the Wicked. When people behave with cruelty, like bullies, they are trying to get attention by creating suffering. Arguing with them or getting angry only fuels their fire. By disregarding the wicked behavior, bullies don't get the response they craved and you suffer less yourself. In fact, by ignoring a bully, you show yourself to be the bigger person.

CLASS ACTIVITY

Pair the students up and explain the four doors and four keys. In each pair, have one act out one of the four doors (behaviors) and the other the appropriate key (approach). They can write simple scripts, and then all the pairs can perform for the group. This will reinforce their understanding of The Four Keys.

Friendliness is the Key to the Door of the Happy

Compassion is the Key to the Door of the Unhappy

Delight is the Key to the Door of the Virtuous

Disregard is the Key to the Door of the Wicked

CHAPTER 9

OVERCOMING ANGER

Mica was enjoying learning about and living yoga. She was developing skills such as compassion, patience, tolerance, and understanding. Yet, things still arose that tested whether Mica really was becoming a true yogi at eight years old.

One day, Fisher was playing kick ball with some other kids on the playground and decided to pick on Isaiah. Fisher coaxed Isaiah into their game saying, "Come on, I'll show you how to play!"

Isaiah thought maybe Fisher was really being friendly, so he joined the game. The first chance he got, Fisher kicked the ball hard, right into Isaiah's stomach, which knocked him over.

Mica saw the whole thing. She ran over, grabbed Fisher by the arm, and yelled, "Why did you do that?! You are so mean, Fisher! A mean, nasty bully!" She was shaking with anger.

Isaiah was still lying on his back in the wood chips. He stared up at Mica as she screamed at Fisher. Mrs. Swan escorted both Mica and Fisher to the principal's office. As Mica recounted what she witnessed to Miss Bell, Mica felt a dirty confusion from her angry outburst cloud her thinking.

The next day,
Mica woke up late and barely had enough time to eat breakfast. With a bagel in hand, she ran for the bus and missed it. "Ugh, power outages!" Mica cursed the morning air waving her fist. Mica's day got worse.

After her mom dropped her off, she realized she didn't have her lunch or her homework. By afternoon, she was feeling anxious and edgy. So, when Fisher decided to shoot a spitball at her in class, Mica lost it. "Fisher! You are such a pig! I hate you!" Mica let go of all the frustrations of her day in one big, loud outburst. Shaken and upset, she broke down into tears.

Again, Mica had let her anger get in the way when she was confronted with an unjust situation or person. So, she decided the following day to make an extra effort to have a good day. She spent extra time that morning in meditation. She used pranayama, or breathing, on the school bus to keep that feeling of openness and calm.

Fisher was enjoying upsetting Mica and was ready for her that day. Mica had made friends with Isaiah after their time together on the science project, and she looked out for him. At lunch, as Isaiah unwrapped his sandwich, Fisher rolled a rotten apple full force right down the center of the table. He laughed wickedly as the apple hit Isaiah's thermos, spilling its contents and shooting rotten apple bits all over his lunch.

Isaiah sat stunned with his mouth open wide.

Mica held her anger in check. She caught herself by taking a really deep breath and exhaling out all the anger in her body. She remembered: "Disregard is the key to the door of the wicked."

Fisher was watching her, expecting her to blow up like she had before.

She caught Fisher's eye as she continued to take deep breaths, then she calmly walked over to the lunchroom supervisor, and told her what had just happened.

Fisher was sent home early with a detention and Isaiah got a free slice of pizza. Mica sat down with a sigh and said to herself, "This felt so much better than getting angry."

CLASS ACTIVITY

Have students record in the journals the times when anger arises and how they use pranayama, or breath control, to help overcome the urge to yell, hit, throw things, slam doors, or lose control in other ways. Do this exercise over a set period of time, and have the students take note of how anger becomes easier to manage.

PART II

SEEING THE GURU

CHAPTER 10

AHIMSA OR NON-VIOLENCE

The man with the long white beard rubs his chin and says:

"Ah, my friends, do you see how Mica has grown? In just a short time, like a well-watered flower, she has grown and is blooming in the radiant light of yoga. Her yoga practice has been a faithful friend. Well, now it is time for Mica to learn more about the teachings of yoga—the yamas and niyamas—starting with ahimsa.*"*

Three years have passed, and Lily was now fifteen years old and in high school, and Mica was turning eleven. She and Mica had hung out at the park, pool, and mall many times, but this was the first time she had invited Mica over for dinner. It was a Monday after yoga class, and Mica was excited to see Lily's house, hang out in her room, and meet her family.

"Welcome, Mica, come on in," Lily's mom said as they went in the house. Class had let out at 5:00, and already Lily's house was filled with the aroma of cooking food. Mica realized how hungry she was.

"We eat early, so I hope you're hungry," Lily said, as if reading Mica's mind.

As they sat down, Mica marveled at all the wonderful dishes. There was brown rice, chickpeas with spinach and tomatoes, a huge salad full of fresh veggies, nuts and dried fruit, and roasted sweet potato.

"Wow, this looks great!" Mica said, filling her plate, "Are you all vegetarians?"

"Well, yeah, aren't you?" Lily sounded surprised.

"Nah, my mom won't let me. I've asked. I love the food at yoga camp, and every summer I come home and ask my mom to cook food like that, but …" Mica's voice trailed off.

"It's a pretty big step, and maybe your mom is just used to cooking a certain way," Lily's mom offered.

"I used to be a big meat eater," Lily's dad added, "but Lily convinced us over all her years of learning yoga that we should become vegetarian. For years,

I had to take blood pressure medicine and had heart disease. My doctor was amazed at how changing my diet reversed my condition. I take yoga classes, too. Yoga is more than exercise, it's a lifestyle."

"What was your motive, Lily?" asked Mica. "What made you decide to make that change?"

"Ahimsa," Lily explained, "is the principle of nonviolence. Eating meat causes suffering to many animals. If I gave up eating animals, just because I didn't like the taste, that wouldn't be ahimsa. It has to come from the right motivation. You need to believe that what you are doing is for the animals, for their well-being, and to stop the suffering inflicted upon them."

"Wow, now I really want to be a vegetarian!" Mica exclaimed. "The thing I did convince my mom to do is buy meat from the farmer's market and not from the grocery store. We've watched all the documentaries, like 'Food Inc.' and read books, like *The Omnivore's Dilemma*, about the devastating affects of factory farms on the animals and the environment. So we buy all of our meat, cheese, yogurt, milk, honey, bread and produce from the local market, from Virginia farmers."

"Well, there then. You *are* practicing ahimsa," Lily said. "The animals raised on small, local farms are treated humanely, allowed to freely roam, and they eat a healthy diet of grass and grain. Even the way they are slaughtered is better, though it is still killing."

"I feel a little better."

"Hey, I have an idea," Lily's mom interjected. "Why don't we have your family over for dinner? I'll spend some time with your mom teaching her some

basic recipes. This might encourage her to make more vegetarian meals."

"I'd *love* that," Mica said, smiling.

Indeed, Mica and Lily's families had many dinners together, and eventually Mica's parents agreed to eat meat only occasionally. Mica, they said, could be vegetarian. As a family they understood ahimsa meant nonviolence in all ways. Refraining from lifestyle choices that cause harm to living beings took some time to get used to, but it felt like the right thing to do.

CLASS ACTIVITY

Choose an age-appropriate book to read about vegetarianism, such as *That's Why We Don't Eat Animals* and *Vegan Is Love* by Ruby Roth, and a documentary to watch, such as "Food Inc.," "What's on Your Plate?" or "Forks over Knives," to educate the students about what is happening to our food and food sources. Visit local farmers and farmers' markets to see firsthand the bounty of food available that supports local business, a cleaner environment, and a healthier lifestyle.

CHAPTER 11

SATYA OR TRUTHFULNESS

The man with the long white beard says:

Now, Mica is ready to move to the next yama: satya *or truthfulness. Never forget, though, that ahimsa is the most important of the yamas.*

Another year passed, and Mica was in seventh grade. As always, Fisher was the class bully. It didn't seem to matter how many trips he made to the principal's office, or how many days he missed for suspensions, he kept on bullying.

Mica overheard some teachers talking in the hall one morning.

Miss Krystall was saying, "… well, his parents have been going through a terrible divorce for years, and Fisher and his brother have been pulled back and forth the entire time."

Mr. Foster concluded, "It's no wonder they struggle so much at school."

Mica felt a burning desire to share this information, but knew it would only be harmful for Fisher. "Ahimsa," she thought to herself. "Nonviolence, not hurting."

But Mica did think it was time for a heart-to-heart with Fisher. She took her opportunity at lunch.

Fisher was sitting by himself at a back table. His black jacket collar was pulled up around his ears and his back was hunched as if to say, "Leave me alone."

"Hi, Fisher, can I eat lunch with you?" Mica asked, feeling brave.

Startled, Fisher stammered, "Uh, I dunno, I guess." After a few minutes he asked her, "What's that you're eating?"

"Fried tofu sandwich with barbecue sauce. It's my favorite."

"*Gross!* I'll stick to my ham sandwich."

Mica cringed, thinking of the suffering of that poor pig that likely came from a factory farm, but said nothing. Eating meat was his choice and his karma. "I wanted to ask you why you pick on people. You know, it just gets you into trouble."

"You gotta be good at something, I guess," he said without looking up.

"Do you know how much you disturb the harmony of our class? How much suffering you cause students, teachers, parents … *your* parents?" Mica had spoken the Truth. She had said it gently, kindly, and with an open heart. Her motive was to help Fisher to become a kinder, more considerate, and less frustrated person.

Fisher shifted in his chair, still not looking at her.

"Hey, I know you have eyes. Let me see them. Look at me."

"I'm not hiding!" He yelled suddenly, startling them both.

Mica said quietly, "Okay, then answer my question."

"I told you already," Fisher saw Mica was beginning to pack up her lunch and took the chance to look up at her. "Why do you care?"

They were finally looking at each other, face to face.

"Because you are my classmate. I've known you since third grade. I care about you as much as I care about anyone else in our class." Feeling she now had his attention, she decided to share what she'd overheard that morning. "Listen, I heard some teachers talking in the hall. You know, Fisher, it must be really hard watching your parents go through this awful divorce."

As if her words had shot him, Fisher's head fell down and his gaze returned to his lap.

She kept going, though. "Do you have anyone to talk to?"

He didn't say a word. Silence.

"Fisher, you can talk to me if you want." She dared to reach across the table and gently touch his arm.

"Why the heck would you wanna be friends with me? I'm the class bully. You said so yourself. The kid with problems at home."

Mica interrupted, "The kid who is smart enough to get better grades. The kid who has all the potential to make himself a kinder person. The kid who could let himself learn to be a friend." She smiled warmly at him.

Fisher found her honesty refreshing after years of experiencing his parents lie, yell, and cheat on each other. Every day for him was a battle. He told her how he had to protect his little brother, Hunter, from the fallout of all that happened at home. The bell rang and Fisher took a deep breath and released a burdened sigh. "You know, Mica, I hear ya. I do. It hurts to hear it, but it's a hurt that helps, and that's different for me."

Mica smiled to her new friend, "Do me a favor, Fisher. Next time you think of doing something hurtful to someone else, think of Hunter. Think of showing him what it means to be the best you can be."

"Well, you know, we're in middle school now, and I guess it's a good time to change things up. Do you think our class could handle a boring old Fisher?" He cracked a smile.

"Fisher, I doubt you'll ever be boring. Letting go of the bully inside you will surely earn you some friends, and you can count me as your first one."

They walked out of the lunchroom together as new friends.

Satya is not just saying the Truth, but also acting it, and doing so with honesty and kindness in the spirit of *ahimsa*, so that your words are coming from your heart and are not hurtful.

Sanskrit word
Satya
"truthfulness"

CLASS ACTIVITY

Sit in a circle. Each person takes a turn sitting in the middle, trying to get someone else to smile by saying, "Smile if you love me." If the person being asked smiles, it is his or her turn to sit in the middle of the circle and take a turn. This is great fun for getting everyone to laugh and feel more connected as a group in an open, honest way.

CHAPTER 12

ASTEYA OR NON-STEALING

The old man says:

The next yama is asteya *or not stealing. Mica had an interesting day learning this lesson. My yogi friends, pay attention to the world around you, for it will teach you many important things."*

It was a Saturday morning, and Mica awoke excited to go on a hike with Lily and some other friends. Lily had just gotten her license and wanted to drive up to Serenity Peak for a day of exploring and hiking the trails. Lily arrived promptly at 10:00. Everyone was supposed to be at Mica's by 10:30. By 10:40, Luca and Samantha had arrived, but Raven wasn't there yet.

"I want to go. Come on, we shouldn't wait any longer," Luca whined impatiently.

"Yeah, I agree," Samantha said.

"Let's give her a few more minutes. She tends to run late," Lily said, looking out the window.

So the girls sat down and looked over the trail map. They plotted the course they would take for the afternoon. Lily looked at her watch.

"Hey, it's almost 11:00 and it's going to take at least an hour and a half to get there. If we don't leave now, we won't have enough time to really enjoy the hike." Lily grabbed for her keys.

Samantha hadn't realized how much time this was going to take. She had to be home for her sister's birthday dinner. "Will we be back before 6:00? My mom is planning on picking me up by then."

"*Ugh!* I guess so. You should have told me before—we could've left earlier. Now Raven has made us so late we'll have to revise our hike." Lily was trying hard to keep her inner calm.

Mica added, "You know, Raven has stolen our day from us by being so late. She could've at least called."

Lily looked at Mica and said, "Asteya."

"What?"

"Asteya, it's one of the yamas of yoga, like ahimsa and satya."

Sanskrit word
Asteya
"non-stealing"

"You guys and your yoga talk!" Raven said bursting through the screen door.

"Raven, you are a time thief!" Lily accused with annoyance.

"A what? I overslept! What's the big deal?"

Mica said, "Raven, every one of us made a point to be here on time. You have made us all wait, and you've messed up our plans for the day. Being late robs people of precious time."

"Wow, I never thought of it that way before. Sorry, guys," Raven said, feeling her guilt.

"Well, now it's 11:20, and we have to be back by 5:30. I tell you what, is everyone free tomorrow?"

Everyone said they could rearrange their plans for Sunday and make the hike.

"Then, I'm leaving *promptly* at 9:00," Lily said, turning to leave. "If you want to go, be here. *I will not wait.* As for today, I'm going home to clean my room. That's what I was supposed to do tomorrow. At least my mom will be happy."

Raven just sat there on the edge of the couch, surprised at how she had spoiled everyone's plans for the day.

Mica leaned toward Raven, whispering, "You know, a phone call would have helped a lot."

Raven sighed, "I'm really sorry I ruined everyone's day. I seem to be forever running late. But I tell you what, I'm going to make an extra effort not to be late anymore."

So, Mica's day was suddenly wide open, and she thought a bike ride would be fun, so she asked Raven to join her. They rode through her neighborhood and into town. Union was a small city with a charming downtown. The streets were lined with brick row houses that had stores on the street level and apartments above. In the center of town was a beautiful park that the Union Garden Club Association kept full of seasonal flowers. In the middle of the park was an antique, ornate merry-go-round. Mica and Raven laid down their bikes in the grass and sat on a park bench to watch the little kids play.

Mica noticed a few older kids eyeing a mother with a double stroller. She nudged Raven, "What are those kids up to?"

"I dunno, but it looks like trouble."

Mica was on her feet and running just as one of the kids grabbed the woman's purse. Without thinking, Mica tripped the boy, who fell flat on his face. The purse landed a few feet in front of him. Raven was a good back up, as she ran and got a hold of a second boy who was going for the purse. A third boy ran away.

In the seconds that all this took place, an officer patrolling the area saw the commotion and ran over. Mica held the first boy down, with one knee firmly in the boy's back. The police officer saw the purse, the struggling boys, and the distressed mother and didn't need an explanation. He immediately handcuffed both boys.

"I can't believe you girls just did that!" the policeman said with disbelief.

The woman said gratefully to Mica and Raven, "Thank you. I had just been to the bank, and all of my vacation money is in my purse."

Raven proudly said, "Black belt, ma'am. I've been doing karate since I was five."

Before taking down their information as witnesses, the policeman said, "Just remember, in many cases such acts of heroism could cost you your lives. If these hoodlums had knives or guns, someone could've been seriously hurt."

The two boys stood there looking really angry. It was then that Mica noticed how dirty they were, how their clothes were worn, too.

Mica said to the one who had grabbed the purse, "Why did you do a dumb thing like that?"

The kids looked at her, and one said, "I just wanted some money. She looks like she's got plenty."

"That's no reason at all! You know *nothing* about me, son," the lady shouted, shaking a finger at him. "My husband and I have saved up for years to take this trip. Mostly, we just get by, and this is our big treat for all our work."

Mica whispered to Raven, "Asteya."

Raven laughed, rolling her eyes. "Ugh! You, yoga people!"

They got back on their bikes and rode home. Raven's mom was waiting when they pedaled into the driveway. She looked really agitated.

"Mom, what's up?" Raven asked, concerned.

Raven's mom worked for *The News Daily*, the local paper. "I had a huge story I was writing about the danger to the future of food because of genetically modified organisms, you know, GMOs. I was talking to a co-worker at lunch about it yesterday ..." her voice trailed off as if her words were continuing silently in her head. "Well, someone must have overheard me. Pete Royal submitted a story *exactly* like mine, and we're both up for the same promotion and only one of us can get it. You know, I left a rough draft of my article on my desk yesterday. I went back last night to get it and it wasn't there. I was supposed to turn it in first thing this morning."

Raven asked, "Is there a way to stop this?"

"It goes to print tonight."

"Let's get down there before it hits the press! Come on, Mom, we still have time to get your article back!" Raven said excitedly.

"You mean steal it back?" her mom corrected.

"What!? How is that stealing?" Raven asked and then interjected looking at Mica, "Hey, does anyone see a theme with this day?"

Mica smiled and nodded.

Raven continued, "Mom, you have the notes, you did the research, the interviews are all on your computer. Call the editor and explain what happened. Why let this go if it means so much to you? And think about it, Mom, do you really want a *thief* in a higher position at your job?"

"Raven, you are *so* right! I'm so glad you talked me through this. I'm going to call her right now." She walked off with her cell phone in hand.

Practicing asteya means not stealing another person's time, belongings, or ideas, as Raven and Mica experienced firsthand during their exciting day together.

CLASS ACTIVITY

Read and discuss a story about stealing, such as Nicola Davies' *The Promise* by or *The Berenstain Bears and the Double Dare* by Stan Berenstain.

CHAPTER 13

BRAMACHARYA OR MODERATION

The wise teacher says:

"Now things get interesting. We will learn about bramacharya. *Yes, it is a big word. It means moderation in all ways: not too much of this, not too little of that, but just enough."*

It was the start of summer vacation, and Mica had planned all week to celebrate with friends. The Friday that school let out, she headed to a pool party, then after, she went over to Sarah's house for pizza and a sleepover.

Mica awoke Saturday morning thinking to herself, "Wow, I am so tired. All that swimming yesterday, all that pizza, all that soda. And what time did we go to bed last night?" Mica rubbed her eyes awake.

Mica looked at her sleeping friend and said, "Sarah, I have to go! I have tennis lessons this morning."

Sarah awoke and rolled out of bed and shuffled toward the stairs, "Come on, let's get breakfast."

"I don't have time. My mom will be here any minute."

So, Mica went from the pool party, to a pizza dinner, to a sleepover, to a tennis lesson. Not surprisingly, Mica did not do well on the tennis courts that day.

Mica got home and found Raven waiting for her on the front porch.

"Yo! Let's go for a bike ride! Isn't it a gorgeous day?"

Mica mustered up a second wind of energy, "Let me grab something quick to eat."

She hadn't had breakfast, and now a banana with a handful of almonds was serving as lunch. A couple hours later, Raven and Mica

stopped by the neighborhood pool. A bunch of their friends were there, so they decided to hang out. Lily arrived all excited about a movie that had just come to the town's theater. "Let's go!"

Before she knew it, Mica was sitting in a cinema between Raven and Lily, watching an action-packed movie. She didn't even realize how hungry she had been until she finished the bucket of buttered popcorn and a bag of licorice candy. This turned out to be her dinner.

That night, Mica slept more than twelve hours. When she woke, she felt awful. Her usual, healthy routine had been replaced by non-stop excitement, with skipped meals followed by junk food. She decided to have a pajama, stay-at-home kind of day. She went downstairs and made sandwiches. Then she plopped down in front of the television to watch a movie. She was still ignoring her routine.

At dinner, Mica ate one helping too many of potatoes, lentil dahl, and rice. Feeling uncomfortably full and dull-headed from hours of television, Mica went to bed early.

"Mica, remember, you start yoga camp tomorrow," her mom called behind her as she went upstairs.

"Great!" Mica tried to sound excited. She loved yoga camp, but she just felt so out-of-whack it was hard to feel enthusiastic about anything.

Monday morning at 8:30, Mica found herself at camp and stumbled in still feeling her energy was off. Miss Nalini and Miss Nitya welcomed her with hugs. The day's lesson happened to be on the yamas of yoga. Now in the teen program, the teachings of yoga philosophy were becoming a bigger part of the camp experience. Mica loved it all.

"So, let's talk about Bramacharya," Miss Nalini began. "This means to practice moderation, which is to not overdo things."

Miss Nitya nodded. "And what happens when we lose moderation?"

Deja answered, "We lose our balance."

"Right! And how do we lose our balance?"

Alejandro said, "We eat too much or sleep too much?"

Miss Nalini smiled and said, "Exactly. Like the way you feel the day after a sleepover with a friend?"

Sanskrit word
Bramacharya
"moderation"

Mica could not believe the irony of this discussion, given the events of her weekend. "Miss Nalini, may I share?" Miss Nalini nodded, so Mica continued, "I spent this past weekend with no moderation. I ate too much or not enough. I ate a lot of junk food or skipped meals, and then overate Sunday dinner at home. I stayed up late or slept too much. And I overdid it on activities one day—I played tennis, I swam, and rode my bike. The next day I just lounged around watching television and movies. For the first time in years, I made no time for my yoga practice. I haven't done hatha or meditation since Friday morning."

"So, how do you feel today?" asked Miss Nalini.

"Look at me!" Mica exclaimed. Indeed, her complexion was pale, she had gray circles under her eyes, and her energy was obviously low. She went on, "I feel gross!"

"Thank you for sharing, Mica, and demonstrating so well what bramacharya is and what happens when we don't follow it," Miss Nalini concluded, leaning over to give Mica a sympathetic hug.

After that lesson, Mica was more mindful of her routine, remembering to maintain balance. She made sure she took the time to eat nutritious meals, she slept eight hours most nights, she kept up her yoga practice, and she learned to say "no" if her day filled up with too much to do. Mica was learning to walk what Buddhists call "the Middle Path" and what yogis call bramacharya: moderation, balance, avoiding all extremes.

CHAPTER 14

APARIGRAHA OR NON-GREED

Now, the last of the yamas is aparigraha. This teaching is about desires. How do you resist craving, wanting, grabbing for things, for money, for control, for recognition? Why are we so tempted to strive for things, even when we have enough?

The old man strokes his long white beard and considers this.

It was Monday afternoon in yoga class, and Miss Nitya was teaching for Mr. Lee, who was planning a summer camping retreat. All of the students were excited about their big yoga weekend together. Mica went home with the list of supplies she would *need*.

Her mom looked it over and said, "Well, Honey, we have some of these things, but you may just have to do without others. We'll figure it out."

Mica felt unsettled about having the right supplies. She even considered how her supplies would measure up to everyone else's. Her cartoon action hero sleeping bag was from first grade. Her mom insisted the sleeping bag was fine, and she was not about to go spend money on something they did not *need*.

"But, Mom! What about hiking boots? I've gotta have those!" Mica said with exasperation.

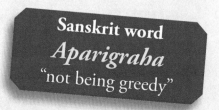

Sanskrit word
Aparigraha
"not being greedy"

"Hiking boots are expensive. Just wear your tennis shoes. They will be fine."

"Mom, this is the supply list Mr. Lee gave us. We *NEED* this stuff!" Mica walked away, feeling her anger was about to get the best of her. Taking deep, releasing breaths, she calmed down and then called Mr. Lee.

"You bring up a good point, Mica. This list should not be a what-is-*needed* list. Heck, we could go out with just the clothes on our backs and have a real roughin' it adventure," he laughed at the idea. "The list is just items that will make your trip more comfortable. Bring what you can, and we'll make do."

Mica really *wanted* a new sleeping bag and hiking boots. Now she had to accept that "making do" with a cartoon sleeping bag and tennis shoes was what she'd have to do.

The following weekend she went to a birthday sleepover party. She reluctantly brought her childhood sleeping bag and was relieved to see many other girls had old sleeping bags, too. Raven even had her brother's old one with trains on it. She couldn't help but laugh at herself for all her worrying.

At the party there was a piñata hung from a tree branch in the backyard. Everyone took turns swinging the bat until the piñata broke open, spilling candy all over the lawn. Some people were fighting over who had grabbed what. "Hey, that was mine!" "I got it first!" "You got more than me—that's not fair!"

Mica was really disappointed in the way her friends were acting. She found a couple of pieces of chocolate and went back inside. Later, as they watched a movie, Mica saw people reaching into the popcorn bowl, taking fistfuls and shoving them in their mouths. It seemed all the snacks were getting grabbed up by greedy hands. "Why is this bothering me?" Mica asked herself.

At the next yoga class, Mr. Lee was back, and Mica took him aside to share what she had observed at the party.

He smiled and nodded.

Mica waited for an answer, but it came during class.

"OM," Mr. Lee brought the class to their mats. "Deep breath in, exhale OM. Keep your eyes closed. Breathe and feel the vibration of OM."

Mica had let the space of OM wash away her worries.

When the lesson began, Mr. Lee told the class, without naming Mica, what she had told him. He said, "My, yogi friends, this is one of the yamas, *aparigraha*. It is about greed. Do you see how, in this series of events, greed took over common sense and even good manners?" He paused, looking at the students, then continued, "Greed reveals itself in many ways, like wanting to have more things than other people, or more control, or more popularity. And often, the more someone gets, the more someone wants, and might do terrible things to get it."

Mr. Lee held up a list and said, "Now, speaking of things people need and want, I'd like to talk about our camping supply list. No one should feel that they *need* to bring all of these things. Most important are a sleeping bag and good walking shoes. Okay?"

The class looked a bit relieved.

Once they were on their retreat, Mica found out that lots of the kids didn't have hiking boots or fancy camping equipment. Mica also discovered

that long weekend in the mountains just how little is really *needed* to survive and still be comfortable. They learned to forage for berries, identify edible plants, use sunlight for a compass, build a fire, and make simple shelters. They enjoyed fresh-picked watercress and dandelion salad with potatoes roasted in

the fire for dinner. Dessert was a bowl of berries. Even clean clothes and a daily shower weren't all that necessary.

Mr. Lee said this was truly living the simple, good life, and that Aparigraha is not just about greediness and hoarding things, it is also a principle about living simply.

They paused after dinner to meditate on the sun setting behind the Blue Ridge Mountains.

Mr. Lee wrapped up the weekend by asking the students to reflect on what they thought simplicity was. "I'd like each of you to meditate on the idea of simple living. Write down your answers and we'll share them in the next yoga class."

Mica did her assignment, and by the fourth day she had an answer:

Simplicity is living with what you need:
a warm safe home, a loving family,
nutritious food and clean water,
enough clothes without too much,
and a regular Hatha yoga practice with daily meditation.

For me, this is living simply and living well.

CLASS ACTIVITY

Piñata Greediness.
Buy or make a piñata in the shape of something inanimate, such as a soccer ball or a pirate ship. Fill the piñata with quarters or nickels (about $25 worth), then hang it from a tree. Have the kids take turns whacking the piñata until it opens.

After the kids grab up all the coins, have them sit in a circle. Ask them what they see as they look around at the other kids. They will see some who have a few coins, some who have a lot, and maybe others who have none.

This is a great opportunity to discuss socio-economic differences in our schools, community, and in the world. Ask what solutions they can imagine for spreading wealth and making life easier for those that have very little? What opportunities do we have for improving our world and the lives of others less fortunate?

CHAPTER 15

CLARITY OF MIND

The man with the long white beard smiles and says:

So, my yogi friends, you have learned a lot about the yamas of yoga, which are teachings you can apply to your own lives. Now we go deeper, observing the niyamas, the spiritual journey of yoga. It begins with saucha, *which is purity of mind, body and spirit.*

Hatha yoga is purifying—it helps cleanse the body of toxins and motivates digestion. A vegetarian diet promotes a calmer mind by nourishing the body without polluting it. Meditation opens the mind to be free of thoughts and distractions.

Mica's thirteenth birthday arrived. As she sat in front of the mirror in her room she recalled how she first learned about yoga when she was eight. Almost five years of asanas, meditation, and being mostly vegetarian had created fertile ground for her to develop in many ways.

To celebrate her birthday, Mica asked Miss Nitya to come to her house and teach a yoga class, followed by a special lunch at her favorite Indian restaurant. She invited all her yoga buddies from class.

Mica could still be just as anxious as she used to be when she was eight. As the time for the party got close, she ran around straightening things, making sure everything was just right. Her mom laughed saying, "Mica, I swear, you're like a tidy little mouse scurrying around this morning. Everything is fine. Come sit down with me."

Mica sat down on the sofa close to her mom.

"Have I ever told you about my short time studying meditation?" her mom asked.

Mica looked up with surprise, "No!"

Sanskrit word
Saucha
"purity"

"Well, it was many years ago when I was at Columbia University. A friend dragged me to the first session. It was a yoga studio in New York City. I wasn't very good at it, and I only went a few times. What I do remember is that the teacher sat with a bowl of clear water that had mud settled at the bottom of it. Whenever someone fidgeted or moved around, he'd stir the water with a bamboo stick, and the water would cloud up."

"That's because when you're not focused and your mind is all over the place you can't think clearly," Mica said.

"Hmmm, well, Honey I was trying to make a point," she smiled, tugging at Mica's shirt.

Mica looked down and saw she was still in her pajamas, "Okay, Mom, I'm busted!" she laughed. "Cloudy-headed, scatter-brained Mica is going to go get dressed and wait for her guests upstairs!"

Mica ran up the stairs and called down, "I think I will also devote some time to meditating my mind back to clarity."

"Good idea, I'll come join you!"

CLASS ACTIVITY

Read the book *Moody Cow Meditates* by Kerry Lee MacLean and then make Mind Jars, following the directions from the back of that book. These jars are like snow globes, and all the glitter represents negative feelings. Explain that when disturbing feelings arise, it's like shaking up the Mind Jar, then demonstrate. Sit, breathing calmly, while the glitter settles back down. In a similar way, sitting in still meditation restores peace to the mind.

CHAPTER 16

SANTOSHA OR CONTENTMENT

The wise man takes a long drink of water and says:

Now, Mica will learn of santosha, which is the practice of contentment and the last niyama we will discuss. Ah, happiness, satisfaction, feeling fulfilled by a simple life. This all comes from you, my friends. It all comes from within you.

Mica was in her Monday yoga class, and a new student was joining their group. Some of the kids in class had grown up studying with Mr. Lee, and others he had invited, like Mica, because he recognized them as undiscovered yogis or kids who would naturally take to the practice.

"Hi, I'm Mica. Have you been doing Hatha for a while?"

"My name is Bella. I've never done—what did you say?—Hatha before. But I've been meditating for years."

After class, Bella and Mica chatted while waiting for their Moms to pick them up. They were becoming great new friends.

Bella invited Mica over one Saturday on a beautiful autumn afternoon. Bella showed Mica the apple orchard in her big backyard.

"Can we pick some?" Mica asked excitedly.

"In a little bit. I thought you might like to sit out here with me. I don't have any friends I can meditate with. This is my favorite spot."

"Um, sure!" Mica said happily, sitting down on the leaf-covered grass. She leaned against a apple tree and closed her eyes. Mica's mind was all over the place. She thought about what her mom had said about the clear water of the mind, Saucha, and purity being necessary tools for meditation.

Mica released a deep sigh. She peeked an eye open in Bella's direction and was startled to see Bella peeking an eye at her, too. They erupted into giggles.

Bella then shared with Mica how she meditates. "I let my body go, focus on the breath, open my mind, and after a while I feel a total sense of freedom." Bella threw her arms open, looking up at the sky and continued, "It's like being

a kite. I throw myself to the wind and let go. I love it. But it took me years to train my mind not to wander."

"Wow. I have a hard time getting my mind to focus on any one thing," said Mica. I've been sitting for years, and it doesn't seem to get any easier."

"No, practice isn't supposed to, as it gets harder you grow more, learn more. It's neat like that. It's not hard like a crazy math equation, but more like the challenge of climbing a mountain."

"What's your mom making for dinner tonight?" Mica asked, changing the subject.

"I don't know. But see, there you go!"

They both erupted in another fit of giggles.

"What *is* that?!" Mica yelled out loud.

"That ever wild monkey mind," Bella answered. "I love how Mr. Lee teaches us all about yoga philosophy."

"I know, I feel lucky to have him in my life," Mica said. "I'm trying to think of the word he uses when we're practicing meditation—san ... san ... *santosha!* That's the word."

"What's that mean?"

"It's about being present, not letting your mind wander to the future or the past, but staying right here, right now."

"Yes," Bella said, "When you think about it, the past is just a memory, the future is a dream, so if all we have is *Now* we might as well enjoy it."

"Let's try that meditation again, Bella," said Mica with renewed confidence, "but this time we will stay firmly focused on 'the Now.'"

"Our breath can hold us here."

"Now, no distractions," Mica insisted, then closed her eyes, leaned back against the tree, and took a deep breath of apple-scented air. For a long while she let go. Mica's body felt as if it were one with the tree, the grass, the leaves, the air, the sky, the Earth herself. Her open mind flew like a bird to the Now, perfect, present Moment.

Santosha.

Sanskrit word *Santosha* "contentment"

CLASS ACTIVITY

Read *Milton's Secret*, a children's book by Eckhart Tolle. Devote some time to meditating on stillness, silence, and breathing in this Now, perfect moment. Sit in meditation for a set amount of time each day and use your breath as a focal point. Journal afterward about the experience.

PART III

BECOMING THE GURU

CHAPTER 17

ASHTANGA YOGA OR THE EIGHT LIMBS

The man with the long white beard says, "Ashtanga Yoga *consists of the principles of the* Eight Limbs *of yoga. What are these limbs, anyway? Is there a tree in yoga? Yes, in a way, there is a tree in yoga—one with branches and limbs. When you climb a tree you reach for the limbs to pull you up, seeking the bigger branches to support your weight. When you can truly*

climb the Tree of Yoga, branches and limbs, you reach the top and are free—Samadhi!"

During Monday yoga class, Mr. Lee had set up a white board that read "Styles of Hatha Yoga" at the top. Once everyone was seated, they took a deep breath for "OM," enjoyed a quiet period of meditation, and then Mr. Lee began class.

"So, before we begin our asanas or poses, I thought I would show you some of the many styles of Hatha yoga. Does anyone know one?"

Bella answered, "My Mom takes Vinyasa classes at this studio."

Shanti added, "My aunt, Gita, is really into Ashtanga."

Joey exclaimed, "My parents are into Ashtanga too!"

"Okay, we have Vinyasa and Ashtanga," Mr. Lee said, writing these on the whiteboard. It would be helpful for your understanding of yoga to take some classes that offer different styles of Hatha. I'm going to give you a brief description of each of the most popular ones, so you can see how they differ and yet are ultimately all *Hatha*."

Mr. Lee wrote:

Vinyasa combines a series of flowing asanas in rhythm with the breath for an intense body-mind workout.

Ashtanga means "eight limbs" and is an intense, fast-paced practice, moving from one pose to the next in a flowing series of specific asanas.

Iyengar is focused on the body's alignment. Poses are held for a longer period of time with the use of props to precisely position the body.

Kundalini combines breath and the asanas with the goal of releasing energy in the body through the seven energy centers or *chakras*.

Bikram, or "hot yoga," is taught in a room set to around 100–120 degrees to loosen the muscles while stretching and intensely release toxins through sweat.

Yin Yoga opens the hips and strengthens the back muscles to allow for greater ease sitting in meditation. The poses are held for several minutes to stretch the tissues around the joints. It is said to be older than most Hatha practices.

Anusara is a new style that is light-hearted, open, free-spirited, and emphasizes physical alignment.

Sivananda is based on five principles: asana, pranayama, relaxation, a vegetarian diet, and meditation.

Integral Yoga follows the teaching of Sri Swami Satchidananda and is a gentle style of hatha with asanas, pranayama, chanting, and meditation.

Mr. Lee counted the list and said, "That's nine styles of Hatha yoga, and there are others. But this shows you there are many approaches to Hatha practice."

Joey asked, "Which style of Hatha have you been teaching us?"

Mr. Lee answered, "I teach Integral Yoga, which is why you may have heard me mention Sri Swami Satchidananda. His ashram is called Yogaville and is near the Blue Ridge Mountains in Virginia."

Mica was curious to try these different styles. She wanted to ask about Yogaville and learn more about Integral Yoga, but now wasn't the right time. Mr. Lee had a lot to cover, and she would have to ask later. Mica thought about how she enjoyed the slower, more meditative approach of Integral Yoga that Mr. Lee taught.

Bella asked, "Mr. Lee do you teach other styles of yoga?"

"Actually, I do. I occasionally teach a Yin class. Would you all like to try that style today?"

The class agreed, and Mr. Lee led them through a short series of poses.

Mica felt herself sinking deeper into each asana. Not aware of the five minutes that went by in each one, she felt her breath quiet along with her mind. Her hips were opening into a deeper stretch, her back strengthening, and her focus was very meditative. At the end of class she felt open, light, and relaxed. Yin yoga was her new favorite style, and she checked out the studio's schedule and found a class she could take.

After class, Mr. Lee asked for feedback. The students so enjoyed learning a new approach to Hatha, that he decided to invite them to try another style,

Ashtanga, at his friend's studio for next Monday.

So, the following week, Mica met her class in front of the Ashtanga Yoga Studio of Union. It was pouring rain, and Mica ran in the double glass doors trying to avoid getting soaked. As she took off her shoes and hung up her raincoat she looked around the room. Incense was burning, filling the air with the sweet, earthy aroma of sandalwood. There was a large, wooden statue of the Hindu god Ganesh angled near the entrance with a tall bamboo tree next to him. On the wall over the Ganesh was a sign that read:

> **ASHTANGA YOGA** – THE EIGHT LIMBS
> *1) Yama* – Self-Restraint
> *2) Niyama* – Observance
> *3) Asana* – Postures
> *4) Pranayama* – Breath
> *5) Pratyahara* – Sense withdrawal
> *6) Dharana* – Concentration
> *7) Dhyana* – Meditation
> *8) Samadhi* – Super Consciousness

Mica sat down on a bamboo bench, took her journal out from her bag, and copied the sign. Mr. Lee peeked out from the classroom and motioned to her to come in. Mica enjoyed the faster pace and the intensity of the class. After Miss Nadine finished teaching the class, Mr. Lee ushered the students back to the front room.

"Mica, what were you writing down?" Mr. Lee asked.

Mica pointed to the sign on the wall. Some of the kids hadn't noticed it.

Mr. Lee asked them to gather around so he could explain it. "So, you all should recognize some of the words on this sign. This first word, yama, is the five practices of self-restraint. What does self-restraint mean?"

Sarah answered, "Self-control."

"Great, and what are the yamas we learned about?"

Sarah continued, "I think I remember them as **aparigraha**, which is not being greedy; **ahimsa**, which is nonviolence; **asteya**, which is not stealing; **satya**, which is being truthful, and the last one …" Sarah paused and thought really hard, but couldn't remember it.

"Oooh, I know, I know!" Joey yelled out.

"Okay, Joey, go ahead," Mr. Lee said.

"Bram … brama … **bramacharya**? The yama of moderation, balance." Joey stammered.

"Yes, very good!" Mr. Lee was pleased. "Next are the niyamas. Who remembers those?"

Aida offered, "The niyamas are about being aware and observant. The niyamas are **saucha,** which is being pure, like eating a vegetarian diet, not getting jealous or angry, and keeping your body clean. The other one you taught us was **santosha**, which is being content, accepting life for what it is."

"Very good, Aida. I'm really impressed, class, by how much you have retained these teachings. I didn't go too far into the niyamas, I just mentioned a couple. Here are the rest.

Tapas   is about staying focused and being disciplined in your practice, avoiding being distracted by extremes, like being hot or thirsty.

Svadhyaya   is the journey of understanding yourself through meditation and self-inquiry.

And finally, it's a big word …

Ishvarapranidhana   is to surrender to God and to trust that the path of your life is guided by a higher power."

Mr. Lee continued, "Now, back to the Ashtanga sign on the wall, we covered **yama** and **niyama**. Who can help us with the rest of the limbs?"

Shanti said, "Well, the **asanas** are the Hatha poses we do in class. **Pranayama** is purifying or cleaning the body with breath control."

Mr. Lee nodded and added, "Right, and then we come to **pratyahara,** which is a pretty intense, advanced practice of not getting attached to external senses. One way to do that is Pranayama which puts all of your focus on the breath, letting go of all your other senses and thoughts. **Dharana** is concentration, as in meditation, where your focus is entirely on one thing, without distraction from what's going on in your mind or around you. **Dhyana** is also about meditation, but more specifically, looking deeply at something in order to know it or understand it. **Samadhi** is the ultimate goal of yoga, just like the word "enlightenment" used in Buddhism. This is the freedom from self and the release into a super-conscious state, free from attachment, desires, or any sense of an individual self.

These eight limbs of yoga are a fairly intense path to walk, my friends. I teach them to you so you can learn all that yoga is, but I certainly don't expect you to fully understand or live it, yet. I will say, though, that by starting at your young age, you have an advantage over most people to develop your practice to a much greater level." Mr. Lee smiled warmly and bowed, saying, "Namaste."

> **Sanskrit word**
> *Ashtanga*
> "Eight Limbs." These are practices that allow you to climb to the top of the "tree of yoga," samadhi!

Mica had a lot to think about as she rode home. She looked at her journal each day, making notes about what she thought of these eight limbs. They did seem advanced, but they also seemed very simple.

She called Mr. Lee over the weekend and discussed some of her thoughts and asked some questions. "Mr. Lee, I think the big message of these eight limbs is to develop ourselves through meditation, breathing, eating a healthy vegetarian diet, doing our asana practice, and refraining from getting caught up in distractions. It's observing, watching, being present, and devoting yourself to a spiritual life."

Mr. Lee asked Mica, "What religious faith is your family?"

"Well, I'm from the Turtle Mountain Tribe of the Chippewa. My family still honors many of the traditions of our tribe, like respecting Nature and the seasons, living an honorable life, and respecting our tribe and all living things. It's hard living so far away from our people, especially my grandmother, Ravenwalk, who I am really close to. But my dad does a good job of keeping us connected. It's important to him that we do not forget our tribal roots."

CLASS ACTIVITY

Try different styles of Hatha yoga and discuss the similarities and differences, while recognizing the common threads that make them all Hatha—the physical aspect of yoga.

CHAPTER 18

BHAKTI YOGA AND HATHA YOGA

We are going to learn more about the Tree of Yoga. *Mica is growing older, and she is experiencing yoga in her life in more meaningful ways. Our tree will teach us about the six branches or paths of yoga. Let's climb up and take a look,"* the man with the long white beard looks up into a large oak tree and smiles.

Mica is now eighteen years old, and she has been learning to live yoga for ten years, with daily meditation, Hatha classes, yoga camps, and field trips. She is a young woman graduating from high school. She isn't sure what to do next.

One night, Mica had a dream about a giant tree. In the tree was a house, and in the house was a person. She wasn't afraid. She climbed the tree, went into the house, and sat down in a corner of the big, open room. Suddenly, the sun broke through the window and revealed a man. He was glowing in the sunlight.

Mica awoke feeling that there was something profound about the man in her dream and felt a strong connection to him. She got up and sat in her meditation chair by the window. She felt the new morning sun on her face and thought, "I must find him. I must know who he is."

At yoga class on Monday, Mica arrived early to talk to Mr. Lee. She told him about her dream.

"Wow, Mica, that is a remarkable dream. You know, maybe it's about the Tree of Yoga."

A newer student, Maya, who just arrived, interrupted, "Tree of Yoga? Oooh, can you tell us more about it, Mr. Lee?"

Mr. Lee looked at Mica, knowing how well she knew this, and then at Maya, seeing how fresh and new a student she was. "Well, the yoga practice is made up of the yamas, niyamas, and the other limbs we've discussed in class, but yoga also has the six branches." He interrupted himself and said, "You know, the timing is perfect. There are six classes left before we break for summer. You'll know all about these six branches by the time we're done."

Mr. Lee took the first part of class to introduce all six branches, writing brief descriptions on the whiteboard. "Remember, class," he said, "the word 'yoga' means unity. Each of the six branches are paths to achieve unity—unity of body and mind, unity with your higher Self, unity with others and with the world around you."

Bhakti – the path of devotion

Hatha – the physical path

Japa – the yoga of chant

Jnana – the path of knowledge

Karma – the path of selfless service

Raja – the path to understand yourself

"As most of you know, yoga is much more than a form of exercise. The physical aspect is just one branch on the Tree of Yoga. It's like art—there's drawing, painting, dance, poetry, music, writing—each is a different path or *branch* of art, but they are all art. In the same way, yoga has many connected paths to unity, like a tree with many large branches."

Then Mr. Lee pointed to the list and asked, "Which branch do you think is of greatest importance?"

The students guessed Hatha since that was the one they knew the most.

The Tree of Yoga

Svadhyaya
Ishvara
Pranidhana
Tapas
Niyama
Saucha
Santosha
Yama
Satya
Ahimsa
Asteya
Bramacharya
Aparigraha

Niyama
Yama
Raja
Karma
Asana
Dhyana
Samadhi
Pranayama
Hatha
Jnana
Pratyahara
Dharana
Bhakti
Japa

"It would seem to be so, but no. It is Bhakti yoga. Does anyone go to a synagogue, church, mosque or temple?" A few students nodded. "Then you have an idea. Bhakti yoga is learning to live with your heart open—a heart open to serve God, Buddha, Allah, Rama, Gaia, or whatever you call the Spirit that speaks to you. It's being inspired by someone greater than you, who inspires you to be better than you already are. You understand?"

Mica added, "And you, Mr. Lee, you are someone like that for us."

"Thank you. Yes, in some ways, I am. Bhakti yoga makes all the other branches come to life. You'll see how as the weeks go by."

The second week, Mr. Lee talked about Hatha yoga. Some of the kids were hoping for something new, because they thought they already knew all there was to know about Hatha.

Mr. Lee began class. "What do you know about Hatha?"

Aida said, "It's the asanas, the poses we do."

"Yes, and what else?"

Desiree added, "Meditation, too, oh, and deep relaxation."

"Good. Asana, meditation, *yoga nidra*, and what else?"

Shanti said, "What about breathing, pranayama."

"Yes, very good, pranayama, the control of breath." Mr. Lee smiled. "So, Hatha yoga is the physical part of yoga. But what would affect Hatha yoga? What things do we do that interfere with our Hatha practice?"

"Skipping practice to watch TV!" Joey exclaimed.

Maya offered, "Staying up too late, which makes you tired."

"Good," Mr. Lee said. "Not minding our schedule certainly interferes with Hatha. What about in our lifesytle?"

Mica said, "Mr. Lee, I remember when I first started learning yoga ten yeas ago. I ate a pretty healthy diet, but I still had the occasional soda, meat, and junk food. Then my whole family became vegetarian. Over the years, I've also learned to curb the desire for soda and junk food. I think a healthy diet is a big part of Hatha yoga."

"Yes, Mica, and why would that be?"

"Well, it's like a clear bowl of water. If the water is your mind, then it's naturally clear and calm. Sugary foods, processed food, fast food, microwaved food, and meat are like pebbles dropped into the water. The mind and body are no longer clear and calm, but agitated, restless and cloudy."

"Thank you, Mica, well said."

Desiree cried out, "Why shouldn't we eat meat? I love chicken and hamburgers!"

"Where does it come from, Desiree?"

"Um, I don't know. You mean, like, cows?"

"Yes," Mr. Lee nodded. "What are cows, pigs, chickens, sheep, deer, crab, shrimp, fish—what are they?"

Bella said gently, "They are living beings just like you and me." She looked around at her classmates. "Really guys, you need to stop and think about what you are eating, where it comes from, and how it was made. Does it cause suffering to others or harm to the environment? We can't continue to blindly shove food in our mouths just because it tastes good or it's what we've always known to eat."

"Okay," Mr. Lee said, "so now you know, but this is also a choice. You can choose to buy from your local farmer's market to reduce pollution and to not support factory farming. You can choose to not eat animals to prevent the suffering they would endure. You can choose to not buy or eat food you know to be unhealthy. Educate yourself and your family by taking the initiative to learn more."

Mr. Lee looked around the room, "I want you to challenge yourselves to not eat fast food, soda or sugary foods for the next few weeks. Then, you tell me how your meditation practice is affected." Mr. Lee knew many of his students already ate very healthy diets, but there were still a few who didn't.

"Lastly, a pure yogi diet is made up of fruits, vegetables, whole grains, nuts, and lentils, with plenty of fresh water. Use your journals to record what you experience in your meditation as a result of improving your diet."

CLASS ACTIVITY

Have the students record in their journals the effects of diet on meditation. Have students explain how their meditation was affected after eating different kinds of food. Did they notice a difference from eating a yogic meal with water in contrast to consuming meat, milk, processed foods and/or high-sugar foods?

CHAPTER 19

JAPA YOGA OR
THE YOGA OF CHANT

The third week, Mr. Lee came to class with drums and other musical instruments. "Today, we are learning about Japa yoga, the yoga of chant. This is kind of like singing your prayers. Chanting is a wonderful tool to use in meditation to keep the mind focused just on what you are singing. Like the sound of OM, chanting traditional Sanskrit awakens a vibration that has many healing properties as well."

Mr. Lee picked up a drum and began to play.

Miss Nitya came into the room and also began playing a drum. Miss Nitya said, "In India, they hold Kirtans, a gathering where people sing sacred chants together. Today we're going to chant one easy song that we can use for our meditation practice."

The students picked up instruments, and Miss Nitya led them in singing "Hari Om." Over and over again, the rhythm of those two little words rolled through the class like great waves. Students closed their eyes and swayed to

the music. As the drum beat went faster and the tempo picked up pace, their voices grew louder. Mica felt as if she were entering a hypnotic state; it felt like she was floating, and her heart was blooming like a flower. Then the chant slowed down to silence. Everyone sat still with eyes closed, instruments quietly held in their hands, and they meditated on the vibration of "Hari Om" still echoing in their minds.

Miss Nitya asked quietly, "So, what do you think of Japa yoga?"

A chorus of responses erupted, "Cool!" "Awesome!" "I can still hear it in my head!"

She continued, "Japa yoga is a tool for meditation. You noticed how you could still hear and feel the music even after we were quietly sitting? The chanting helps hold your focus. The chanting can also be devotional: it can be a song of praise, worship, or gratitude."

Mr. Lee added, "Do you also see how Japa yoga is an integral part of Bhakti, the devotion aspect of yoga?"

Mica shared, "I felt my heart open like a flower."

Mr. Lee continued, "Yes, a heart open to the world causes no harm. Rather it makes the world better, because your love is poured out to every living thing around you." Then he held up a notebook and asked, "Now, does everyone have their journals? We've used them over the years for our practice, but they will be an especially important part of next week's lesson. Please journal daily about who you think you are. Ask the question, 'Who Am I?'"

Miss Nitya said, "I've kept a journal since I was ten years old, it is a dear friend to me always. Journaling isn't just a way to record what you do every day, but more about what you experience and feel. As you journal, think about who you are, ask questions, sit in silence, and look deeply into yourself."

Mica loved journaling and writing down her private thoughts about her practice, her feelings, and what was happening in her life. She loved her teachers and how they encouraged her to dig deep and discover all that she was.

Mica went home that day and sat on her front porch. For a long time Mica held a meditation, still focused on the sound vibration of "Hari Om."

When she opened her eyes her mom was standing in front of her smiling. "I love you, Mom," Mica said and stood up to give her mother a big hug.

Mica thought to herself, "This is yoga."

CLASS ACTIVITY

Break into groups, and have each group create its own chant. The groups can choose known tunes, like "Row Row Row Your Boat" or "You Are My Sunshine," and chant words they find inspiring, such as Peace, Love, or Joy. Perform these chants for an audience (or for each other) and mix in some traditional chants, such as "Om Nama Shivaya" or "Om Shanti." Allow time for meditation after each chant so everyone can experience the afterglow of the vibration.

CHAPTER 20

JNANA AND RAJA YOGA OR THE DISCOVERY OF WHO YOU ARE

On the fifth Monday, the students were ready with their journals. Mr. Lee opened class with a question, "Who would like to share how they began to discover who they are?"

Mica volunteered, "I wrote in my journal everyday, asking myself, 'Who am I?' I meditated on the question. I took long walks. I sat with my family. I hung out with my friends. I did my schoolwork. The whole time, I was aware of my Self asking that question. After a week, I feel like I have a pretty good idea of who I am, but I want to learn more, do more, experience more."

"Yes! And this leads to Jnana yoga: the quest for knowledge, wisdom, truth!" Mr. Lee was very excited. "It is also Raja yoga, the search for understanding your Self. Raja involves the Eight Limbs and means 'royal.' You have already begun your journeys down the royal path through the yamas, niyamas, asanas, journaling and meditation. Raja brings knowledge of your True Self, while Jnana is the path to find out more about yoga, life and wisdom through reading the yoga classics like *The Bhagavad Gita* or *The Upanishads*. I've brought some copies for you all to borrow, if you like. I will warn you: this is not light reading, but there is great benefit in learning the stories and teachings of the ancient Gurus."

Mr. Lee placed a pile of books on the desk at the back of the room. Then he returned to his mat and continued, "All of your life is a journey, but to make it even more meaningful, to truly walk the path of yoga, to really live yoga, you will learn who you are through Bhakti, Japa, Hatha, Raja, Jnana, and Karma, the six branches of yoga."

Bella asked, "What is Karma yoga? Is that like 'What goes around comes around?'"

Mr. Lee answered, "Yes, but more than that. I will meet you all at Mission Park next Monday for our final class. For now, let's do some Hatha together."

Mica felt heaviness in her heart. This was it. She was heading into the last class with Mr. Lee. She was graduat-

Sanskrit word
Jnana
"knowledge"

ing from high school. The idea seemed like a dream, but the time was getting closer, and she couldn't help but feel some of her old anxiety creeping in.

That night, Mica had another dream of a man in a tree house. He was looking at her. She could see his mouth moving. What was he saying?

Mica awoke and got out of bed. The full moon of early June lit up the front lawn. The air drifting through the open window was still cool. She sat in her meditation chair and looked at the moon. She asked in a sleepy whisper, "Who are you? Why are you in my dreams? I feel such a connection to you. How can I find you?"

CHAPTER 21

KARMA YOGA
OR THE YOGA OF
SELFLESS SERVICE

Monday morning, Mica prepared herself for her last class with Mr. Lee. After school, she took the bus to Mission Park. It was a low income, run-down area of town. Mr. Lee was waiting with plastic bags and gloves for everyone.

"Take a look around, friends. What do you see?"

Desiree said, "I see a mess! Look at all this trash!"

Mr. Lee said, "I see a park. Let's make it shine!"

So the yogis spent the rest of the afternoon into early evening cleaning up the park. They had a box for recycling and filled over a dozen big, black garbage bags. Just as they were sitting down for a rest, Miss Nitya pulled up in a van. She got out and waved them over. They all began to set up tables and chairs.

Mica wondered what was going on when another van drove up. Miss Nalini brought out pans of hot food and placed them on the tables. The students were truly perplexed, then Mr. Lee ended the mystery by announcing, "Let's invite our neighbors to dinner!"

"What?!" Joey blurted out.

"Yes, these people are our neighbors. This park is our park. This city is our city. This country is our country. This world is our world. We are all one big family. Karma yoga is the path of service, helping others without waiting to be asked, and without any thought of a reward. No one asked us to come here today. No one will thank us or give us a citizen's award. We did this because, why?"

Bella answered, "Because it is the right thing to do."

"Exactly. And look around you. Look at the difference you have made to this community. How do you feel?"

Mica said, "I feel good. I feel like I made a difference, and it does feel really good!"

"Let's go then."

Mr. Lee and Miss Nitya took the students in two groups to knock on the doors of the small neighborhood and invite people to join them in the park for dinner. Soon, a line formed by the tables. The students helped serve the food. It was a wonderful vegetarian meal with lots of fresh, local produce donated from the growers at the farmer's market. The yogis were there to serve, not to eat.

At the end of the day as the sun was setting low in the sky, the students sat down in a circle with Mr. Lee, Miss Nitya, and Miss Nalini. Not one kid had complained about not eating dinner or being tired. They all had shared in a very powerful experience. The neighbors were so happy and grateful, and their gratitude was all the reward anyone could have hoped for. The class sang a joyful round of "Om Shanti," a chant for peace.

Miss Nalini smiled and said, "Wow, what a great day. Namaste, friends!" She bowed deeply.

Mr. Lee bowed and said, "Namaste. I love each of you dearly. I hope you have learned how to live yoga, how to live with your hearts open to serve others, to share with others, to see the world as a place where you can make a difference."

Miss Nitya smiled and bowed, "Namaste, friends. The Light in me bows to the Light in you. I know I will see some of you at yoga camp next month. Keep up your practice. Be well."

Mica gave Mr. Lee, Miss Nalini, and Miss Nitya each a huge hug. She cried with sadness for leaving, but also with deep gratitude for all she had learned from them. Mica was ready for what would come next in her life, even though she had no idea what that was going to be.

Mica went home and began to pack.

CHAPTER 22

MICA PACKS TO LEAVE

After Mica's graduation, days after school was finished, Mica's mom walked into her bedroom, "Honey, where are you going?"

Mica looked up with tears on her face, "Nowhere." She tried to force a smile and then stopped packing for a moment.

Her mom sat on the bed with her and said, "Oh, Honey." They held each other there for a while.

"I just don't want to go to college right now. That's why I didn't apply. I feel called to go somewhere else. I just don't know where that is."

"Honey, you have done so well with your schooling, but I've known that going to college right away wouldn't be the next step for you, not now anyway. As much as your dad and I want you to go, this has to be your decision. So much of your school years has been influenced by your yoga, and it seems to be a real passion for you."

"It is, Mom. The more I practice, the more I feel it's what I'm supposed to do. I just don't know where to go from here."

"Well, knowing you, when it is time, you will." Her mom gave her a big hug before letting her go. As a mother, this was a very difficult time for her,

too. The time for her daughter moving away was very close.

Mica heard her mom going downstairs, and again tears fell as she continued her packing. Looking around her room, Mica felt the sense that everything
in her life was about to change.

After dinner, the doorbell rang. Mica's brother ran to answer it with Mica close behind him.

There was Miss Nitya. "Hi Mica. Sorry, I know this is last minute, but I thought you might like to join me for an adventure. Are you busy tomorrow?"

"No, I'm not busy. I'm actually …" Mica didn't know why she was about to tell Miss Nitya she was packed, but she felt her packing had something to do with where they were about to go.

"I've decided to surprise you with where we're going. Pack for camping, but also bring your yoga whites."

"Yoga whites?"

"Oh, yeah. Yogis wear white clothes to special events. You'll see. I'll pick you up at nine o'clock."

Mica dreamed again of the man in the tree house. The tree changed into a beautiful lotus flower, the color of flamingo feathers. This time she heard the man's voice, loud and clear.

He said to her, "Sing, Mica. Sing the song of God!"

CHAPTER 23

THE JOURNEY ENDS AND BEGINS

When Miss Nitya picked her up that next morning, Mica felt that she was going some place very special, a place she would return to again and again.

As they drove south on Interstate 95, Mica dozed in her seat. Miss Nitya rolled down the windows when they turned off the highway and onto the smaller country routes toward Buckingham County, Virginia. Mica opened her eyes and took deep breaths of the fresh summer air. The road snaked around farms and fields and forests before the car slowed. Mica looked to her left, and there was a sign that read, "Welcome to Yogaville."

"Are you serious? This is a town for yogis?" Mica cried out.

Miss Nitya laughed, "Yes, very much like that, Mica. I'll show you around." She pulled the car into the parking lot, leaving the windows down and all of their stuff in the car as it was. Mica shot her a worried look.

"Everything is safe here."

Mica smiled at Miss Nitya as they began to walk past some buildings, a large open grassy area where a few people were playing Frisbee, then off the sidewalk toward the woods. Miss Nitya led the way down a steep path. Mica stopped to look at little piles of rocks neatly placed by the roots of some of the trees. She knew this was a magical, spiritual place. At the bottom of the path they came to a paved road. Miss Nitya was watching Mica for her expression as they rounded the bend.

In a large clearing was a huge, pink, lotus-shaped building rising up from a tranquil lake. Mica's eyes widened, and her face radiated tremendous joy. She could find no words.

Nitya told the story of the LOTUS, Light of Truth Universal Shrine, that was built in 1980 and of Sri Swami Satchidananda, who came to the United States in 1966. "That was the year I was born, a long time ago. The path of Integral Yoga developed by Sri Swami Satchidananda, *Gurudev*, as we affectionately call him, recognizes all religions as leading to One. I'll give you a tour."

They kicked off their sandals at the door by a rushing waterfall and went inside. The cool air conditioning felt good on their hot, sticky skin, the silence filled their ears, and they went into a large, circular room. The walls of the room were filled with display cases with items that represented traditions from each major religion and even the lesser-known religions, such as Wicca and Baha'i. There was even a space to honor the religions that are unknown.

Then they went up a tight, steep stairwell to the top of the LOTUS. The dark room was illuminated by a vertical, white beam of light in the center of the room. The light beam went to the ceiling, where it radiated into many thin, red lights that descended the arched dome, connecting to symbols of each of the major religions on the walls around them.

A loud bell chimed, and Mica looked at Miss Nitya, who answered her silent question, "It's time for noon meditation. Every day at this time, the people of Yogaville are invited to meditate. Would you like to join me?"

The glowing, grateful smile on Mica's face was her answer.

The energy in the room was cool and calm. Mica felt a deep sense of peace and belonging fill her as she meditated. The hour passed like a whispered breath, and when Mica opened her eyes, she knew she was where she had been packing to go. "Miss Nitya, I am home." Tears welled up in Mica's eyes, her heart felt full of light, and goose bumps tingled from the top of her head down to her toes.

Miss Nitya looked at Mica and said, "I know. I have another special place to show you. Come on." Together they walked a straight path away from the LOTUS, past the gift shop and through the parking lot, then up a steep set of steps toward a glass-walled building that sits nestled in a hillside. At the door they slipped off their shoes to respect the yoga tradition of not wearing shoes indoors.

Miss Nitya whispered, "This is the Chidambaram Shrine, dedicated to Gurudev, and there is a life-like, wax statue of him inside. Would you like to sit before him?"

Mica nodded eagerly.

Mica walked slowly, mindfully into the room. She turned and looked up and saw the man with the long white beard—the man from her dreams! Again

she heard his voice, but there were no words, only the sound of OM. Mica knew she'd never be lost again. Gurudev had always been present in her heart. She had felt his presence through Mr. Lee and Miss Nitya and Miss Nalini. She knelt before him and let silence roll over her.

After a while, Miss Nitya motioned for them to leave. As they walked away from the Chidambaram Shrine and back up the mountain path, Miss

Nitya told Mica, "You know, I never met Sri Swami Satchidananda in person, either. I missed many opportunities when I could have. He passed on in August of 2002. I became a yoga instructor in 2006. I will tell you, my greatest spiritual awakening happened here at Yogaville. Gurudev is with me every time I lead Kirtan, every time I teach, every time I am here. It is by his grace that my life has purpose and vision. When I learned to live yoga, I learned what it meant to truly live."

"Thank you, Miss Nitya, for all of this: for sharing your story, for bringing me here. I'm going to go home and finish packing. This is where I'd like to stay for a while."

"You can do that. They have residency programs. You'll learn all about Karma yoga for sure. Plus, you can get certified to teach."

"Oh, I'm *definitely* going to learn how to teach yoga," Mica stated confidently.

So, after lunch, Mica and Miss Nitya enjoyed an afternoon touring the rest of Yogaville. Before dinner, they changed into their yoga whites.

The Saturday program included Kirtan, which is sacred Hindu chanting, and then Satsang, a spiritual teaching on yoga philosophy. For Satsang, they played a video on a large screen of Sri Swami Satchidananda giving one of his talks. Mica sat fixated on Gurudev's voice. She heard his every word. When the video was finished, she was hungry to hear more.

At the end of the night, Mica noticed a salmon-colored chair at the front of the room. She asked Miss Nitya, "Why is that chair left empty?"

"That's Gurudev's chair."

Mica went up and knelt before it. She took a deep breath and closed her eyes. Miss Nitya knelt beside her. Mica took Miss Nitya's hand and, squeezing it gently, said, "He's here. I can feel him everywhere. In one of my dreams, I heard him tell me to sing the song of God."

"Well, then," Nitya said, "you must take a yoga name. *Gita* means the song of God. Would you like to be given that name?"

"I'd be honored! Is *Nitya* your yoga name?"

Miss Nitya nodded with a warm smile. "When I went through my Integral Yoga teacher training, at graduation I was given the name Nitya, which is Sanskrit for 'Eternal One.'" She laughed and added, "Kind of deep, isn't it? But that's the point of a yoga name—it's a name that you grow into."

"That's what we do in our tribe," Mica replied. "When we reach a certain age, the elders give us a new name that reflects the qualities that they see we will grow into."

So Mica took the name Gita, but it would be quite a while before she could use her new name.

When Mica returned home with Miss Nitya, she was overjoyed with what she had discovered at Yogaville. Her parents, though, had other plans for Mica. After she had finished telling them about her amazing adventure, her mom spoke, "Mica, what you have shared with us today is wonderful. Truly, Miss Nitya has opened your eyes, and you now see your future goals very clearly. That is truly a blessing. But, I need you to understand ..." she paused and looked at her husband, who gently put a hand on her knee, "that as much as we would love for you to pursue becoming a yoga instructor and living at

Yogaville for a year, we need you to go home to Nebraska first."

"Mom, why?!" Mica was heartsick with this news.

Her mother began to cry, and so her father continued, "Mica, your grandmother, Ravenwalk, is very ill. We just got a call today that she needs constant care now. Your family needs you to return to Nebraska to care for her."

Mica looked into her lap as she held back tears. Many emotions flooded her mind and her heart as she sat silently. Then, after a few minutes had passed, Mica said, "Okay. I will go to Ravenwalk and care for her as you have asked." Mica realized at that moment how long it had been since she had last written to her grandmother and hadn't seen her in quite a while.

This was no easy task for Mica. In the coming months as she cared for her grandmother, she had to learn how to apply her yoga knowledge in a whole new way. She got up at dawn to do her Hatha practice. By keeping her heart open and her focus firmly on Karma yoga, she was able to care for her grandmother with compassion and unconditional love. She bathed her, fed her, dressed her, sang to her, and told her all she knew about yoga. She listened as Ravenwalk shared her stories of the Chippewa people.

There was very little time for herself, and Mica found that meditations arose on their own during the long spells when she was sitting by Ravenwalk's bed, holding her hand. It was an exhausting time, but Mica learned to be strong and focused on the task at hand.

It was a bitter cold morning in late February, when the snow was still deep and the sky a sheet of palest blue, that Mica awoke to the sound of birds. She had overslept for the first time and missed her Hatha practice. Groggy

with sleep, she threw on her bathrobe, slipped on her boots, and ran outside.

The sky suddenly seemed black with cawing ravens, and Mica noticed that for the first time in days the sun was shining. She stood alone looking at the morning sky and felt the landscape exhaling her grandmother's last breath. She knew it was time to go say good-bye.

She went back inside, leaving the chill of the morning behind her, and entered Ravenwalk's room. Mica leaned over and kissed her grandmother on the forehead ever so gently, just as her grandmother had always kissed her.

That was the day that Ravenwalk died. Mica stayed for days after, helping prepare for the burial ceremony, cleaning up the house and finding her own way to say good-bye. It all seemed so final, as if a door closed that would never be opened again.

Now, more than ever, Mica understood her journey into yoga and how important this time with Ravenwalk had been. Mica decided to remain in Nebraska for some time, teaching herself how to paint the landscapes of the Chippewa Nation. She attended art college the following fall and became a respected artist in the community.

Many years later, Mica found herself back in Yogaville for teacher training. Her life now felt complete as she began leading chanting workshops and teaching yoga. Her favorite part of teaching was working with children, sharing with them what her teachers, Mr. Lee and Miss Nitya, taught her years ago. She created yoga stories for her classes that took young students on Hatha adventures. When it was time for meditation, a character would appear in her stories to guide her students into their sitting time. It was the man with the long white beard.

He is with us always.

Jai Gurudev!

Jai!

GLOSSARY

ahimsa /ah-heem-SAH/   Nonviolence (literally: "non-harming").

ananda /AH-nan-dah/   Bliss.

aparigraha /ah-pa-ree-GRAH-ha/   Non-greed (literally: "non-grabbing"), includes non-hoarding, non-coveting; one of the five yamas.

ashram /ASH-ram/   A community devoted primarily to spiritual teachings and practices under the guidance of a teacher.

Ashtanga Yoga /ash-TAN-ga/   Yoga of the "eight limbs," which are the practices that lead yogis toward samadhi.

asteya /ah-STAY-ah/   Non-stealing; one of the five yamas.

Bagavad Gita /BAH-gah-vad GEE-TAH/   Ancient Hindu scripture in which Arjuna learns the principles of Yoga from Lord Krisna.

bramacharya /BRAH-ma-CHAR-yah/   Self-restraint, balance, moderation; one of the five yamas.

Brahman /BRAH-man/   The Supreme Consciousness or God.

chakra /CHA-krah/   Any of seven energy centers within the body, from the base to of the spine to the top of the head. Chakras can be focal points in meditation.

dharana /DA-rah-NAH/   Concentration; one of the eight limbs.

dhyana /dee-YAH-nah/   Meditation; one of the eight limbs.

guru /GOO-roo/   Teacher or spiritual guide (literally: "remover of darkness").

Hatha Yoga /HA-tha/   The physical practice of yoga, consisting of postures, breath control, meditation, deep relaxation, and diet; one of the six branches of yoga. (literally: "sun-moon").

ishvara–pranidhana   /ISH-va-rah prah-nee-DA-na/   Devotion to a higher consciousness or God; one of the five niyamas.

Japa Yoga   /JAH-pa/   Chanting traditional Hindu songs as a tool for meditation and connection with the Divine; one of the six branches of yoga.

jaya or jai   /Jey/   Victory.

Jnana Yoga   /YAH-nah/   The yoga of knowledge through study of ancient scriptures, such as the *Bagavad Gita* or the *Upanishads*; one of the six branches of yoga.

Karma Yoga   /KAR-ma/   Selfless service to other living beings (literally: "action" or "doing"); one of the six branches of yoga.

mantra   /MAN-trah/   Repeated sounds or Sanskrit "seed syllables" to help focus the mind (literally: "mind-steadying").

niyama   /NEE-yah-ma/   Observances of the spiritual journey of yoga; one of the eight limbs.

Om   /OHM/   The ultimate sound vibration of the universe.

prana   /PRAH-nah/   The vital energy of the body.

pranayama   /PRAH-nah-YAH-ma/   The control of the vital energy of the body through breath; one of the eight limbs.

pratyahara   /prah-TYA-HA-rah/   Sense control; one of the eight limbs.

Raja Yoga   /RAH-jah/   The "royal" path of self-understanding and self-mastery through the eight limbs; one of the six branches of yoga.

Ram   /RAHM/   A name for the Cosmic Consciousness or God.

samadhi   /sah-MA-dee/   Contemplation or the achievement of super consciousness, the ultimate goal of yoga; the last of the eight limbs.

Sanskrit   /SAN-skrit/   The ancient language of India.

santosha   /SAN-toe-shah/   Contentment or satisfaction with circumstances without grasping for more; one of the five niyamas.

satya   /SAHT-yah/   Truthfulness; one of the five yamas.

saucha   /SOW-cha/   Purity of mind, body and spirit; one of the five niyamas.

shanti   /SHAHN-tee/   Sanskrit for peace.

Sri   /shree/   Prefix in names to show respect, especially to venerate a deity or spiritual teacher.

sutra   /SOO-trah/   A saying or teaching (literally: "thread").

svadhyaya   /SVAHD-YA-yah/   Spiritual study; one of the five niyamas.

swami   /SWAH-mee/   Someone who gives up living for material gain in order to learn and teach spiritual values; general term for an advanced teacher of yoga.

tapas   /TA-pahs/   Accepting but not causing pain (literally: "to burn"); one of the five niyamas.

Upanishads   /oo-pa-nee-SHADS/   The final section of the Vedas, which teaches about cosmic unity (that "we are all One").

Vedas   /VEY-das/   Ancient Hindu wisdom literature.

yama   /YAH-ma/   Restraint or self-control in order to live a virtuous life; the first of the eight limbs.

yoga   /YO-gah/   The union of the practitioner with the Ultimate Consciousness (literally: "union" or "yoke").

yoga nidra   /YO-gah NEE-drah/   Deep relaxation or wakeful sleeping (literally: "unified sleep").

REFERENCES

The lessons and philosophies within this book were derived from the Sutras of Patanjali, referenced from the following resources: *Inside the Yoga Sutras: a Comprehensive Sourcebook for the Study and Practice of Patanjali's Yoga Sutras* by Reverend Jaganath Carrera (IYS) and *The Yoga Sutras of Patanjali* translation and commentary by Sri Swami Satchidananda (YSP).

Chapters 1–2

IYS: Pada 1, 1.2: "*Yogas chitta vritta nirodha*. The restraint of the modifications of the mind-stuff is Yoga."

Chapter 3

YSP: Pada 1, 4: "... But without any identifications, who are you? ... When you really understand that, you will see we are all the same. If you detach yourself completely from all the things you have identified yourself with, you realize yourself as the pure 'I.' In that pure 'I' there is no difference between you and me."

Chapter 4

YSP: Pada 1, 3: "Your Spirit self is unchanging, it is indestructible, it is everlasting. How do you see your self?"

Chapter 5

YSP: Pada 1, 1.7: "The sources of knowledge are direct perception, inference, and authoritative testimony"

Chapter 6

YSP: Pada 1, 1.14: "Practice becomes firmly grounded when attended to for a long time, without break, and with enthusiasm."

Chapter 7

YSP: Pada 1, 1.15: "Nonattachment is the manifestation of self mastery in one who is free from craving for objects seen or heard about."

YSP: Pada 2, 2.7: "Attachment is that which follows identification with pleasurable experiences."

YSP: Pada 2, 2.8: "Aversion is that which follows identification with painful experiences."

Chapter 8
YSP: Pada 1, 1.33: "By cultivating attitudes of friendliness toward the happy, compassion for the unhappy, delight in the virtuous, and equanimity toward the nonvirtuous, the mind-stuff retains its undisturbed calmness."

Chapter 9
YSP: Pada 2, 1: "Accepting pain as help for purification, study of spiritual books, and surrender to the Supreme Being constitute yoga practice."

Chapters 10–14
YSP: Pada 2, 2.30: "Yama consists of nonviolence, truthfulness, nonstealing, constinence, and nongreed" (respectively: *ahimsa, satya, asteya, bramacharya, aparigraha*).

Chapters 15–16
YSP: Pada 2, 2.32: "Niyama consists of purity, contentment, accepting but not causing pain, study, and worship of God self Surrender" (*saucha* = purity; *santosha* = contentment).

Chapters 17–23
YSP: The "Eight Limbs" of Ashtanga yoga are: *yama* = self-restraint (Pada 2:29–31, 35–39), *niyama* = observance (Pada 2:29, 32, 40–45), *asana* = postures (Pada 2:29, 46–49), *pranayama* = breath (Pada 1:34; 2:29, 49–53), *pratyahara* = sense withdrawal (Pada 2:29, 54–55), *dharana* = concentration (Pada 2:29; 3:1, 4, 7, 8), *dhyana* = meditation (Pada 1:15; 2:29; 3:1–4, 7, 8), *samadhi* = super consciousness (Pada 1:17, 18, 41–51; 2:2, 27, 29, 45; 3:3, 4, 7, 8, 11; 4:29–32).

The six "branches" of yoga include: *Karma* (selfless service), *Bhakti* (devotion), *Japa* (chant), *Jnana* (seeking knowledge through the Sutras), *Raja* (the quest to understand your Self), *Hatha* (the physical aspect of yoga that includes asanas, pranayama, meditation, deep relaxation, and diet.

CHIPPEWA RELIGION

Many Ojibway people still practice the time-honored Midewewin religion. Midewewin means "Great Medicine Society" and has been an organization of medicine healers for centuries. The priests of the Midewewin contend that their religion began with their cultural hero Nanabozoho, the Great Hare, by order of the Great Spirit. Members of the Midewewin believe that Mother Earth is a living being, and that all plants and animals upon her contain a spirit that is part of the Divine Creator. The Chippewa respected the cycle of seasons, the four corners of the earth, and gave thanks. Aside from being a religious philosophy, the Midewewin preserve the knowledge of the medicinal qualities of plants to aid the people's health and longevity.

The ethics of the Midewewin religion are simple and comprise the structure of Chippewa values. Midewewin philosophy is Nature-centric. Tribal members considered all life to be a family, and lived accordingly. They honored the Four Orders of Creation: earth, plant, animal, and human. Without the first orders, the latter orders (namely humans) could not exist. The Chippewa believed they were the last form of life created on Mother Earth, and therefore they often call other forms of creation their elders. In their value system, respect is one of the greatest virtues. The Chippewa believed a long and balanced life was acquired through following the sacred teachings of the Midewewin.

The practice of the Midewewin instilled values to the individual and the tribe. Characteristics such as sharing, honor, and learning throughout ones life were attributes of proper conduct. The survival of Chippewa society depended on the success of the tribe as a whole. Cooperation was an important factor to maintain safety and well-being for everyone. Individuals were encouraged to develop personal skills. Through observation, members acknowledged another's abilities and honored them. In this way, individuals built self-esteem and a strong sense of pride in oneself and in one's family.

SOURCE: Chippewa tribal website, accessed 2012

For more information about *Yoga with Nitya* products and services,
including the Yoga with Nitya DVD, visit

www.YogaWithNitya.com

For books and other media by The Arival Media and its partners
regarding mindful living and personal transformation, visit

www.TheArrivalMedia.com

Made in United States
North Haven, CT
23 June 2023

38138304R00082